"You want a housemaid, not a wife!"

Thrown into confusion by a bitter argument with her fiancé, Susan fled to her aunt's farm in Hampshire to sort out her future.

But strange accidents started happening. Two horses she was taking care of suddenly died. Someone tampered with the flooring of a nearby construction site and she nearly plunged to her death. When a home-made bomb demolished her car, Susan had to face the fact—someone wanted her out of the way...permanently.

But what could she do against an invisible enemy? Trap him? Her only recourse was to wait for the killer to strike again....

Other
MYSTIQUE BOOKS
by SUZANNE CLAUSSE

Motive for Revenge

by SUZANNE CLAUSSE

MYSTIQUE BOOKS
TORONTO•LONDON•NEW YORK
HAMBURG•AMSTERDAM•STOCKHOLM

MOTIVE FOR REVENGE/first published August 1980

Copyright © 1980 by Worldwide Library.
Copyright © MCMLXX by Librairie Jules Tallandier, as
L'INOUBLIABLE NUIT.
Philippine copyright 1980. Australian copyright 1980.
ISBN 0-373-50091-2

Chapter 1

The April afternoon was unseasonably warm, and as Susan left the art gallery where she worked, she was grateful that she hadn't worn anything heavier than a long-sleeved cotton dress under her trench coat.

The gallery was in Mayfair, one of London's most fashionable areas, and she decided to saunter down Bond Street instead of walking directly to the subway. If she window-shopped for about an hour, she thought, she might to a limited extent avoid the worst of the commuting crowds. It was just after five, but the late-spring sun was high in the sky, as if defying the popular belief that English weather consists entirely of rain.

The exclusive dress and jewelry shops on Bond Street had always held a fascination for Susan, who never tired of gazing into the opulently dressed windows. The prices, of course, were exorbitant, but that never seemed to stem the flow of people rushing in and out of the shops. *I'll bet they're all tourists,* Susan thought wryly, *I'd be surprised if many English people could afford to buy anything in the shops around here.*

Bond Street was congested, and Susan had trouble walking through the throngs of people without occasionally bumping into some of them. With her umbrella held close to her side, she made resolutely for her ultimate destination, the Burlington Arcade. It was a beautiful arcade, and the quality of the shops' merchandise there was wonderfully understated. There were tobacco shops, woolen shops, antique jewelry shops.... Susan continued to stroll along, soon becoming oblivious to the jostling bodies around her. Her face would light up in pleasure when she saw an object of particular beauty—an emerald green Shetland pullover or an antique cameo ring in an exquisite setting, for example.

"Lovely day, isn't it?" the man closing up the tobacco shop asked her.

Susan looked up with a start and smiled her agreement. "They say it's going to be lovely tomorrow, as well."

"Let's hope so, miss."

"E-excuse me," Susan impulsively called after him as he was about to close the shop door behind him. "How much is the Dunhill pipe—the one behind the tobacco?" She pointed as well as she could into the window. Making a face at his response, she thanked him with a rueful smile and began to walk in the direction of Burlington Gardens, the street that was just north of the arcade, and that ran behind the Royal Academy.

Maybe I'll exhibit my paintings here one day, Susan thought dreamily. "How glorious it would be to be paid for your hobby," she said to herself, not realizing she had spoken aloud until one passerby looked at her with a startled expression. Susan smiled back at the man. "An artist's prerogative!" she called to his receding back.

An artist...was she really, she wondered. Did

her humble attempts at painting constitute art? More to the point—would they ever? Susan's expression grew pensive as she continued her walk, but her introspection vanished as soon as she found herself in front of the window of her favorite gallery. She gazed in wonder at the painting displayed there. *Now how does he get such subtle gradations with acrylic,* she thought to herself. *The shading of the blue into green is fabulous!* She continued to stare at the painting in the window for a few minutes longer, then looked at her watch, gasping in surprise as she realized it was well after seven.

Pausing for a moment to figure out which subway stop was the closest, Susan then hurried in the direction of Green Park—marginally farther away, perhaps, but not nearly as packed with people as was Piccadilly Circus. When she got there she hastily bought an evening paper, then caught the next train, relieved when she was able to find a seat. *I'll be glad when all this commuting is over,* she thought. *Oxford will be so peaceful—no subways, no commuters, no hysteria. Just a few more months to go....*

"You're late this evening, darling," her mother said, as Susan wearily walked into the front hall of the Baker house.

"I know, but the time just disappeared. I thought I'd be clever and avoid the rush-hour crowds, but I rather overdid it, I think!"

Mrs. Baker smiled indulgently. She was aware of her daughter's habit of browsing through the art galleries of London. "See anything you liked?" she asked.

"A terrific acrylic," Susan replied. "It was in the window of a gallery in Burlington Gardens. They just opened a new group show, apparently." She headed for the stairway.

"Dinner's in five minutes, darling," Mrs. Baker called, "an if you're going up to your bedroom, there's a letter from Oxford on your dresser."

"What? Already?" Susan gasped, taking the stairs two at a time.

In no time she was up in her room, throwing her coat on the bed and reaching for the letter on her dresser. Tearing open the official-looking envelope, she quickly scanned its contents. Then, her stomach in a whirl, she read the letter again as she slowly sank onto her bed, oblivious of the crumpled coat beneath her.

"Susan, dinner!"

"Be down in a minute," she called back absently.

"Sue, honey?" Mrs. Baker called a minute or two later. "We're waiting for you."

Slowly Susan walked down the stairs and into the dining room, where both of her parents as well as her sister looked at her expectantly.

"Well, Susie?" her sister, Hilary, prodded. "What'd they say? I've been dying of curiosity ever since mom told me you'd got a letter."

"It...it seems they don't want me. I...wasn't accepted."

"Oh, no!" Hilary cried in disbelief. "That can't be! Your marks were fine...there must be a mistake...."

"It appears not," Susan replied in a flat voice, looking at her sister. "The letter said quite bluntly that my academic achievement was not up to their requirements and, naturally, I would understand that with the severity of the competition...." Her voice petered out and she stared at the plate of food in front of her.

"Everyone knows how tough those Oxbridge exams are, darling," Mrs. Baker said gently. "Don't be too upset. There are hundreds of other art schools and universities—"

"But that's the only one I wanted, mother," Susan said defiantly. "You know how much I wanted to go! I've been up there—how many times—to look at the college and...and get a feel for the place. I had my heart set on it."

"I know, honey," her mother said soothingly. "I only wish we could do something for you. I know how you had your hopes up."

"I hear the University of Exeter has a good fine arts course, Susie," her father said gruffly after a few minutes. "Fancy a few years in Devon? I don't suppose you're too late to get in there, if you shake a leg."

"I know, daddy," Susan said, trying to stop the tears from gathering in her eyes. "A friend of mine from school went to Exeter and loved it, but...."

"But what, Susan?" her father asked, putting down his knife and fork and regarding his daughter intently.

"Oh, I just wanted to go to Oxford, that's all. Oxfordshire is so lovely, and the colleges of the university so old and...and historic. I had visions of painting them....Oh, I know it sounds silly and childish and...romantic, but it *is* what I want. Somehow, Exeter—anywhere—pales in comparison."

"So, what do you think you'll do now, Sue?" Hilary asked practically. "You could blow your savings on a trip to Greece. Set up your easel on Mykonos or Santorini...."

"I think Susan can do without your advice for the time being," Mrs. Baker admonished her younger daughter. "No doubt with a little reflection she'll come to her own conclusions."

"Excellent lamb, Sheila," Mr. Baker said, smiling at his wife. "Anyone care for seconds?"

Susan was grateful to her father for steering the subject away from her failure of the Oxbridge entrance exam. She was further gratified when Hilary obviously took the hint and began to chatter animatedly about an amusing incident that had happened at her secretarial college that afternoon.

As SHE LAY in bed that night, Susan's thoughts raced in circles, centering on one central theme: she wasn't going to go up to Oxford that fall. In her mind's eye she pictured the main street, the Broad, and imagined herself walking along it, then over to Magdalen College where she saw herself setting up her easel on the bank of the River Thames. . . . There were deer in the grounds behind Magdalen, quietly left to wander and graze as they had for centuries.

Susan then imagined herself packing up her paints and brushes, stowing them in her satchel, and walking back to the Broad, at peace and in harmony with the venerable old buildings around her. She entered The Nose Bag with its steamy, noisy atmosphere an authentic tea house, and a popular meeting place for students. After ordering a pastry and a cup of aromatic tea, she headed toward a crowded table, acknowledging the waves of her friends. . . .

You'd better stop thinking about it, Susan, she said to herself firmly. *You'll only make yourself more miserable.* Tearing her thoughts away from Oxford, she turned restlessly, readjusted her pillow, and resolved to address herself to the future. What was she going to do? She hadn't made any alternate plans, she had been so sure that Oxford was going to accept her. Go to Greece Hilary had suggested. Susan remembered that she had once mentioned to her sister that she would love to spend a year on one of the Greek islands. The summer before, she had gone to Greece for three weeks with a schoolmate and had instantly fallen in love with the stark cliffs, the whitewashed houses and the *plakas* in the villages. Greece. . . it wasn't such a bad idea, Susan thought wryly. She had felt very strongly that one day she would go back.

Of course, I could keep working at the art gallery, she reasoned. *I could save even more money...but what for? It will seem like such an anticlimax.*

Peter would be pleased.... With a start, Susan realized that it was only now that she was giving him any thought. Dear Peter...she was fond of him, of course; perhaps even more than fond, but she was finding him—she cast around in her mind for the right word—a little stuffy recently.

He still maintained that Susan would be wasting her time by going to university. "Pretty girls don't need university degrees," he'd once told her. And try as she might, Susan had never been able to make him really accept that while she may not have *needed* it, she wanted it.

"Semantics, my love," he would respond, "mere semantics. Why would you want a degree if somewhere in your mind you didn't think you needed it?"

Susan had come to realize Peter had an unshakable belief: women who wanted and intended to have families could most usefully spend their premarriage years in learning the arts necessary to homemaking.

"Of course I want you to use your head, darling," he had said soothingly when she had accused him of wanting a housekeeper instead of a wife. "With your brains, you surely appreciate how much intelligence and ingenuity has to go into the making and running of a home."

On that occasion, as on many others, Susan had admitted that an art college would probably give her a far more useful eduation than Oxford would. But she had wanted to study art history, and the best art history courses were taught at Oxford....

Yes, Peter will be delighted, Susan mused, and with that thought sleep overcame her at last.

Chapter 2

The next morning, listless and tired, Susan dragged herself down to the bus stop at the end of the street. Though at first oblivious to the clear blue sky and to the promise of another beautiful day, she was gradually affected by the tang of the morning air, and by the time she reached the bus stop she was feeling considerably more alert. She actually found a seat on the bus, but the subway train was positively jammed. By the time Susan arrived at the gallery, she was again feeling as subdued as she had the night before.

"Morning, Sue!" Nick, one of the other staff members, called out as she was hanging up her coat. "The coffee's on. Can I get you a cup?"

"Thanks, Nick, I'd love some."

Her voice must have sounded as flat as she felt, for Nick looked at her carefully as he handed her the cup. "What's the matter? You look awful."

"Thanks again!" Susan smiled in spite of herself. "I just heard a bit of bad news last night, that's all."

"Let's have lunch today; you can tell me all about it," Nick said, trying to cheer her up.

"That's sweet of you, but I'm meeting Peter for lunch."

"So I lose out again to the competition, eh?" Nick said, spreading his hands in mock despair.

"Well, Peter's a bit more than that, actually," Susan said with a thin smile. "We're sort of engaged."

"What do you mean, 'sort of'? Either you are or you aren't."

"He...Peter...well, I know he wants to marry me, and we've been going out for ages—"

"Can't talk now, love. Guess who's just walked in? I'll see you!"

Susan turned around and saw the owner of the gallery, so with a nod she took her coffee and walked over to her desk.

The morning passed quickly, and Susan realized by lunchtime that she hadn't given a single thought to anything other than cataloging the Ming and Tang vases in the gallery. She was pleased that her concentration had been so deep that she hadn't thought about Oxford, but as she put on her coat to meet Peter, she realized that her entire lunch hour would probably be spent talking about the very subject she didn't want to think about.

"I CAN'T SAY that I'm sorry, darling," Peter said as they pondered over the menu at a nearby restaurant. "You know my feelings on the subject."

"Yes, Peter, but do you know mine?" Susan asked, a challenge in her tone.

"I should—we've been over the subject a hundred times."

"If by that you mean you've voiced your opinion to me over a hundred times then, yes, I agree," Susan said, closing the menu in front of her and raising her dark blue eyes to Peter's face. "It occurs to me, however, that you don't really understand what it is I want to do."

"Tell me what you want to do," Peter replied indulgently, an almost patronizing smile on his face.

"I want to experience the history of that university, Peter. It's so old, and so...so venerable. I just want to...to be in that environment for four years. It was important to me."

"And I play the devoted fiancé, I suppose, driving up there every other weekend or so...."

"What's wrong with that?" Susan asked impatiently. "It's no great distance, for heaven's sake."

"Calm down, Susan. This is a senseless discussion, anyway. After all, you're not going and that's that. Why don't you apply to an art college? There are plenty right here in London."

"If I had wanted to go to an art college," she answered tautly, beginning to lose her temper, "I would have done so when I left school."

"It seems to me it's the only logical thing to do now," Peter pointed out mildly, after giving the waitress their orders.

"I guess so," Susan said, suddenly deflated. "I must say, though, it's hard to get excited about the prospect. Going to an art college in London seems...dreary, almost."

"I'll tell you what, darling," Peter said briskly. "Let's get married this summer!" He pulled his date book out of his pocket. "Let's see, where are we now? Tuesday, April tenth.... How about, say, August tenth? That Saturday would be the eleventh. What do you think?"

Susan looked at him intently, aware of the doubts and conflicts in her mind. "Are you suggesting that a wedding might put the idea of university out of my mind, Peter? What about after the wedding, when we're married—what then?"

"Then you'll be financially secure, darling, and you won't have to worry about qualifications.

You'll be able to go to any art college that pleases you. I'm making quite good money, you know," he added proudly.

"There's a flaw in your argument, Peter. Why would I want to go to art school any more after we're married than I do now?"

"You're flogging a dead horse, Susan," Peter said, obviously tiring of the subject. "Let's just leave it. The point is you weren't accepted at Oxford. Since you are, therefore, going to be in London anyway, why should we wait to get married? Let's get on with it!"

"You seem very sure of me," Susan said coolly. "I haven't actually said I'll marry you yet. I think we still have a few differences to resolve."

The young man looked at her in dismay. "But darling...."

"It seems to me we've both made rather a lot of assumptions in our relationship, Peter." At his mystified expression she continued, "I assumed you'd be all for me going to Oxford; I assumed you thought it was as important for women to have careers as I think it is. You assumed I wasn't really serious about university, and you...you assumed I'd marry you!"

"You knew my intentions, Susan," Peter said defensively. "You knew I wanted to marry you. We've talked about it before—in general terms, I agree—but still—"

"Let's just wait, shall we?" Susan gently cut in. "There's no rush. As you say, I'm not going anywhere." She picked at her shrimp salad, waiting for Peter to speak.

For a moment or two they ate in silence, then Peter said carefully, "I respect you enough as it is, you know, if that's what you're worried about."

"What?" Susan asked, perplexed. "Respect me for what?"

"You seem to think you have to go to university just to prove something to me."

"For heaven's sake, Peter! I'm not proving anything—to you or anyone. I simply want to study art history!"

"Calm down, Susan," Peter said, uncomfortable at her outburst. "People are staring at us."

"So what? If they'd overheard the remark you just made, they'd probably realize why I am upset!"

"Susan!"

"God, you're smug, Peter! Smug and...narrow-minded!"

"You're getting hysterical!"

"Since my hysteria," Susan said, standing up and tossing her napkin on the table, "is obviously an embarrassment to you, I'll excuse myself. Good-bye!" Gathering her coat in her arms she strode out of the restaurant, all but knocking into a couple of businessmen at the door. With a muttered apology, Susan ran down the street toward the gallery.

"I KNOW what you mean, but you must admit he's terribly good-looking!" Hilary said that evening, as Susan narrated to her what had happened at lunch. "Peter *is* straitlaced, though—even for an accountant!"

"He is attractive, Hilly, I know," Susan concurred. "Sometimes I think I'd like to frame him! Always so beautifully dressed, perfectly turned out...."

"Now, Susan," Hilary warned, "don't start that. You used to adore that very aspect of him—his sophistication, his style...."

"You're right again," Susan smiled. "But some of his views...they're archaic! I tell you, Hilly, I'd be a lot happier with a less handsome face and a more up-to-date outlook!"

Hilary sat for a moment in silence watching Susan,

who was seated at her dressing table, unpin the chignon that kept her hair out of her face at her work.

"Guess who I saw today?" Hilary said suddenly, breaking the silence. With barely a hesitation she answered her own question. "Lindy Barwick!"

"Lindy!" Susan echoed. "My gosh, how long has it been since the last time we saw her?"

"Let's see," Hilary said. "I would say about seven years ago. She's closer to my age than to yours, and I think I was about twelve when she left; you would've been about fifteen."

For a moment both sisters thought back to their summers at their aunt and uncle's farm in Hampshire. Long-limbed, red-haired Lindy Barwick had been one of their summer crowd, one of the group of children with whom they had played while growing up.

"What a temper she used to have," Susan recalled. "She was okay, I guess, but she was moody and withdrawn at times. I remember thinking that it would be only a matter of time before I got on the receiving end of one of her tantrums."

"I did once," Hilary said with a shudder. "It was awful!"

"Whatever happened to her? Where did she go?"

"Don't you remember? Her father was in the army and he got posted abroad. They were sent to Brussels, I think, and Lindy spent her summers there."

"And they've just come back?" Susan asked.

"Only Lindy has: her parents are in Cairo now. I tell you, I got the whole story of her life! When Colonel Barwick got posted the family sold their house in Hampshire. I guess they figured they'd be gone a long time. Anyway, Lindy said she hated Cairo and so she came back here to look for a job instead of staying with her parents."

"Is she job hunting in London?"

"Actually, no. She said she was in London only to do some shopping for her mom—things that Mrs. Barwick can't get in Egypt. Lindy wants to find work in Hampshire, or so she said."

"Why on earth would she look there for a job? I presume you mean out in the country and not in one of the big towns."

"That's what she led me to believe. She said she wants to settle down near where she used to live. I guess she could get a job in Farnham itself," Hilary added reasonably, referring to the village that formed the closest shopping area to their aunt's farm.

"Well, good luck to her. And now, my dear Hilly," Susan said, "I'm going to ask you to remove your beautiful feet from under my quilt, your sylphlike body from my bed, and yourself from my room. It's after midnight!"

THE NEXT two days passed smoothly enough, though Susan still felt subdued. The sharpness of her disappointment had worn off, leaving only a dull lassitude in place of her usual cheerfulness.

At dinner that Thursday evening, the Baker family was in the middle of an animated argument about minority rights when they were temporarily silenced by the sound of the front doorbell. Susan, who hadn't taken a very active part in the discussion, went to the front. Standing on the front stoop was Peter Whitelaw, and Susan was inwardly amazed to notice that he seemed self-conscious.

"Hello, Peter," she said coolly. "We're just about to have coffee. Will you join us?"

"I guess I'm a bit early," he said, looking at his watch. "I thought we might go over to The Rising Sun and have a drink. But if you're still eating. . . ."

"Why don't you go ahead? You're bound to see a couple of your friends, and I'll meet you there in about half an hour."

"Are you sure? I mean, if you'd rather...."

"I'll meet you in half an hour," Susan repeated firmly. "See you later." She shut the door as he turned away.

"Do you know," Susan said, returning to the diningroom table, "I do believe Peter looked ill at ease just now. In all the years I've known him, I've never seen him look uncomfortable before."

"He must take after his father, who's quite a cool customer," Mr. Baker offered. "I've done business with him from time to time, and he always seems very sure of himself."

"Peter looked almost...flustered tonight," Susan remarked.

"I'll bet he's getting himself into a real state," Hilary laughed, "wondering whether you'll apologize or else say you don't ever want to see him again!"

Hilary's chuckle seemed genuine and for the first time in a long time Susan took a long, objective look at her younger sister. Hilary was a younger, slightly paler version of herself. She had the same rich, dark hair, but her skin was more an ivory than a peach color, and her eyes were a light, clear blue, rather than the dark, opaque blue of Susan's. Slightly shorter but proportionately as slim, Hilary bore a striking resemblance to her older sister, and both girls were obviously their mother's daughters.

Hilly loved London, Susan knew, and had never expressed an interest in doing any extensive traveling outside of Britain. When her secretarial course was finished she would have all the skills necessary to be a top-notch secretary. She dressed beautifully and had a streak of no-nonsense pragmatism in her that was quite foreign to Susan.

Hilary had made it quite plain to Susan that she thought her going to Oxford at twenty-two years of age was a silly thing to do, but if that was what

Susan wanted, then she wished her the best of luck. Hilary herself was happy at secretarial college. At nineteen she was in her second year and due to complete her course the following month. "The way I see it," she had once said, "a person who can type pretty well owns the world. Until we're computerized out of business, everyone's going to need secretaries!"

I could use a little of that practicality myself, Susan thought wryly to herself. *In fact, Hilly and Peter would be a much better couple than Peter and I are!*

THE COOL NIGHT AIR collided with the hot, smoky atmosphere of the pub as Susan opened the front door of The Rising Sun and looked around for Peter.

"Over here!" she heard him call and slowly she made her way through the tables to the corner where he was seated. He introduced her to the friend he was sitting with, Philip Turnbull, and then Philip went off to the bar to get her some wine. Susan slid onto the bench next to Peter.

"I wasn't sure you'd come," Peter said a little diffidently after the other man had left. "But now that you're here, I think we should clear the air. You gave me quite a jolt at lunch the other day, Susan. I don't think I've ever seen you lose your temper like that."

"Well, Peter, I'm afraid I'm going to give you another jolt. I'm leaving London tomorrow night after work, and I don't know when I'll be coming back."

Chapter 3

The mechanics of her plan had been easily worked out. Susan had phoned her aunt, Ruth Coleman, early the next morning and had invited herself down to her aunt's farm for an unlimited stay. She had explained to her family that, if she couldn't go to Oxford in October, Hampshire in April was the next best thing. With a cheery farewell, as well as promises to phone and to write, she had gone off to work carrying her heavy suitcase.

She had managed to sooth the owner of the art gallery by agreeing to call her sudden departure a leave of absence. She was touched that he was pleased enough with her work to be willing to hire her back whenever she wanted to return to her job.

As the train chugged wearily out of Waterloo Station, Susan felt suddenly exhausted. The first elation that came from her sudden decision had vanished, leaving her with the unsettling feeling that of all the mistakes she had ever made, this one might, without a doubt, be the most rash.

But by the time she arrived at the Farnham station an hour or so later, Susan found that she was really looking forward to being in the country again. She had packed her paints and sketchbooks, as well as her jodhpurs and riding boots. If her time was taken up with riding and painting and helping her aunt on the farm, Susan realized with a tinge of excitement that the days would pass quickly and pleasurably.

Aunt Ruth, Susan's father's sister, had come to meet the train, and she quickly enveloped Susan in a warm hug. Then she stood back and looked at her niece.

"Hello, and welcome! What a pleasure to see you! And you'll have to tell me what prompted your visit." Ruth Coleman, despite her happy marriage, had remained childless. Since her husband had died two years ago, she had made no secret of her loneliness. Having her brother's children stay at the farm every summer had always been a pleasure and a delight to her, and she had more than once expressed her disappointment that they no longer visited for such long intervals as they used to. Ruth was a good-looking woman, fine featured like her brother, but Susan noticed the pencil-thin lines of sadness on her face—lines that hadn't been there before Uncle Frank had died.

"Oh, a change of scenery, Aunt Ruth, and a yearning for country air!" Susan answered lightly, deciding to wait awhile before she told her aunt about her failure to get into Oxford and her subsequent argument with Peter. "I've missed you!" she added impulsively, and suddenly realized how true the statement was. Her aunt had always been like a second mother to her and Hilary—a "summer mother."

"Well, love, I'm delighted to see you, and you know you can stay as long as you like. I find the house is a bit quiet with just myself for company, and I'll be glad to have you around."

There was no self-pity in Ruth Coleman's voice, and perhaps because of that, Susan suddenly felt guilty at not having spent more than the odd weekend with her aunt in the last four years. Had it really been that long since she'd spent a whole summer on the farm? She put her hand on her aunt's and gave it a squeeze. "I'll try and stir things up a bit then, shall I?"

RUTH DROVE her little Mini along the winding country road, shifting gears with the ease of someone who knows a route well. "Nothing's changed much, really," she said in response to Susan's query. "Without Frank I can't manage much more than the five thousand guinea fowl I've got, what with the turkeys as well. The local farmers help me out a lot, bless their hearts, but the bookkeeping alone takes up a fair bit of my time. But you know all that. Let's see...." She paused to consider whether or not there were any recent events that might interest her niece.

"How are Richard and Gilly Evans?" Susan asked after a minute. "I heard their parents died. Are they still in the big house or did they sell it?"

"No, they still have it. Gilly's still at school, you know. She's what...about fifteen or sixteen now, I guess. Richard thought it made sense to keep the house, so that Gilly would have somewhere familiar to come back to during the holidays. When she's finished school he'll likely reconsider selling it—though I know both he and Gilly adore it. He's fixed the place up a lot—put on a new roof, and so on. He'd do just as well to hang on to it if you ask me."

They fell silent once again, and Susan studied her aunt's profile. The older woman looked preoccupied and Susan commented on it.

"Nothing serious, love," her aunt said with a smile. "Old Lucy Whilsmith is laid up with a broken hip and she asked me to get her a few things in town. Mind if I drop you off at the farm and then I'll continue on to her place? I won't be long. By the way, did you know her niece is back?"

"Yes, Hilly mentioned she'd run into Lindy earlier this week in London." Susan didn't tell her aunt that it was their conversation about Lindy Barwick that had given her the idea of coming to Farnham herself.

"Lucy's not pleased, I can tell you," Ruth went on in her direct way. "She's not like me, Susan, you see. She's older, for one thing—more set in her ways. She likes her privacy and is in no mood to have Lindy move in. Lucy still writes, you know, and she hates having her solitude interrupted."

"But Lindy will look for an apartment somewhere, surely," Susan protested.

"We'll see; she's been here for ages already," Ruth replied. Susan didn't comment further.

Soon they were going down the driveway of Grasshopper Hill, the Coleman farm. "You know, I don't think I've been here for a year . . . yet now that I'm back, I feel as if I'd never left!" Susan exclaimed.

"Welcome home, Susan," her aunt said affectionately. "And I'll see you in a little while."

Susan heaved her suitcase out of the trunk of the car and waved to her aunt. She went around to the kitchen door, and just as she reached it, she heard an excited barking. Then Willie, Ruth's Irish wolfhound, came bounding up the path from the vegetable garden. The dog greeted Susan exuberantly, and it was all she could do to stay standing—on her hind legs, Willie was practically eye to eye with Susan. "Hello, old thing!" she laughed. "I keep forgetting how big you are."

Reaching the door latch and getting inside with Willie still jumping around for joy was no small feat, but finally Susan got into the kitchen and took off her coat. Shoving her case to one side, she went over to the stove to make herself a cup of tea.

The kitchen was just as she remembered it—gleaming white walls and woodwork and sparkling modern appliances. The enormous wooden table in the middle of the room was surrounded by six straightback wooden chairs with cushions on them, covered in the same pretty blue and white floral material as the curtains. The Colemans always ate most of their meals at this table, saving the dining room for guests and more formal occasions. Lively discussions, confessions, complaints—there weren't many subjects that hadn't been aired around that table—the true center of the house.

With one hand gripping her mug and the other dragging her suitcase, Susan made her way up the polished wood stairs and into the bedroom that had always been hers. The familiarity of the room sent a wave of nostalgia through Susan, even though her absence from Grasshopper Hill hadn't been unusually lengthy. As she heaved her case onto the bed, she noticed with amusement that the fluffy eiderdown was awry and that there was a slight depression in it, the size being comparable to the spread-out form of a very relaxed wolfhound who was still convinced she was a lap dog.

Susan quickly changed her woolen suit for a pair of jeans and a shirt, eager to expose her bare skin for the least possible amount of time. As usual Ruth had left the windows wide open, and the room, although fresh and well aired, had a distinctly chilly feel to it.

As she put her makeup case on the dressing table, she noticed for the first time the framed photograph beside the little vase of petunias her aunt had thoughtfully placed there. "Where on earth did she find this?" Susan murmured. The picture was of six smiling teenagers, all dressed in

jodhpurs and riding jackets and holding up ribbons
of various colors. "I'd forgotten about that horse
show," she murmured again. "It seems ages ago—
five or six years, perhaps?" Gilly Evans was in the
foreground, the youngest of the group by some
three or four years. Behind her stood Hilary, Lindy
and Susan, all looking very proud. In the back row
were Richard Evans and Lindy's brother, Anthony.
Susan squinted at the photo. Richard must have
been about eighteen then. He had light brown hair,
bleached blond by the sun, and the long, lanky
frame of a natural athlete. She remembered that
his eyes had always been a startling, unusual green.
Looking at the picture she recognized that familiar
smile—the easy, confident smile of a competent
performer who's accustomed to winning.

Turning away from the dresser, Susan looked
out the window onto the expanse of green lawn
that was framed like a picture by a luxuriant rose-
garden border, and she let her mind wander back to
those golden summers. She had known Richard
and Gilly ever since she could remember. Though
Richard had been two years older than Susan, they
had always been firm friends, riding horseback and
playing tennis together. Even during the winter
months, when each of them had been away at
school, they had exchanged the occasional letter.

Then Susan had met Peter—urbane, sophisticated and studying to be an accountant. She had
been swept off her feet, and suddenly she had lost
all interest in going to the farm. During the entire
summer vacation before her last year at school, she
hadn't visited her aunt even once. Richard had been
down to Farnham from Cambridge, she knew, but
galloping over the common seemed a poor substi-
tute for going to wine bars and bistros in the company of handsome Peter Whitelaw. Hilary, who
had visited Aunt Ruth as usual that summer, had

mentioned that Richard had asked after her. With some embarrassment Susan now recalled her answer: "For heaven's sake, Hilly, it's so boring at the farm. I can't believe Richard still finds Farnham entertaining! Doesn't he have any sophistication at all?" Well, Susan thought, feeling her face grow warm at the memory, Hilly got rid of my airs and graces fast enough. Her sister had teased her relentlessly until Susan had had to laugh at herself.

"Ah, youth!" Susan sighed. She'd been pretentious and, no doubt, insufferable that summer. She had adopted all of Peter's opinions, repeating them ad nauseam to the family every day. Her mother's indulgent smiles on such occasions had infuriated Susan, who had hotly accused her mother of insensitivity to her blossoming maturity.

It was probably just as well that Richard hadn't seen her during that period of her life, Susan concluded guiltily. He'd likely never have spoken to her again.

"Susan? Susan!" The sound of Aunt Ruth's voice interrupted her reveries, and she came back to the present with a start. Shadows were drifting into the room and she glanced at the clock on the dresser. She'd been standing at the window for nearly half an hour! Hastily pulling on a sweater, she ran down the stairs and into the kitchen where Ruth was putting the kettle on.

"Sorry, Aunt Ruth—I didn't even hear you come in," Susan confessed as she went to help with the dinner. "I guess I must have been daydreaming."

"Never mind, dear, you'll get used to country life again in a few days. Now we have to decide on a couple of things. First of all, is there anything special you want to do while you're here? If there is we should make arrangements. And secondly, what do you want for dinner?"

Typical Aunt Ruth, Susan thought happily. *While*

I'm dreaming my life away she's as practical and thoughtful as ever. "The answer to both questions is nothing special," she said out loud.

Ruth laughed. "In that case, it's paint the turkey coop and spaghetti," she said, her dimples showing her appreciation of her niece's easygoing attitude. "The painting can wait for the next sunny day, but we really should get going on the spaghetti."

The two women worked in companionable silence for a while, their movements coordinated from many summers of working together in the farm kitchen. Susan hummed contentedly as she sprinkled oregano into the tomato paste, and by the time she finished dicing the celery she was whistling. She looked up to find Ruth eyeing her speculatively.

"Feeling better?" the older woman asked gently.

Susan blushed. "I never could keep any secrets from you, could I?" she said. "I'll make you a deal, Aunt Ruth—no questions till supper's ready, okay? Then I'll tell you all about it."

"All right, dear. And I think we should make this a special occasion. After all, it's your first night here in what seems like years. Why don't you go down and get one of your uncle's bottles of wine? God knows why I've saved them for all this time— they're probably covered with dust; that is if all the corks haven't popped out.... Anyway, we'll have a real Italian meal, wine and all."

Susan found her aunt's gaiety contagious. "It's a deal," she said, and headed for the cellar, humming.

BY THE TIME Susan finished telling Aunt Ruth about Oxford and Peter's devastating comments, the bottle of wine was almost empty. The two women were both feeling a little flushed as Ruth got up to clear the table and Susan put the kettle on for coffee.

"What we have to do," Ruth said, enunciating rather carefully, "is to formulate a plan of attack."

"Attack? Attack whom?"

"Attack on two fronts," Ruth went on, as if she hadn't heard her niece's question. She set the spaghetti platter down very gently on the counter and began filling the sink with hot, soapy water. "First, we have to find some things for you to do."

Susan groaned. She had learned, at the tender age of thirteen, that Ruth had very definite ideas about keeping busy. Cleaning the entire farmhouse was a morning's work to the older woman; she would finish the house, mow the lawn, muck out the turkey coop and then—just to keep her hand in, as she put it—she'd tackle the attic, or the barn, or put in four hours doing research about something at the local library. Susan saw her visions of horseback riding and painting start to rapidly disintegrate.

"Aunt Ruth . . ." she began hesitantly, not wanting to criticize the woman's attempts to help.

"Don't you Aunt Ruth me, Susan Baker! I know what you're thinking—you're thinking I'm a workaholic. Well, you may be right, but you don't have to worry. I have no intention of turning you into a handyman."

Ruth paused for breath, watching as the steam began to curl from the spout of the shiny old kettle. "I think we should let those dishes soak for a while, don't you? Let's just enjoy our coffee and work out a strategy."

Susan began turning the handle of the antiquated coffee grinder, forestalling any possibility of conversation for a few moments. The grinder, mounted on the wall next to the refrigerator, was extremely noisy. Ruth had always joked about being thankful that her nearest neighbors lived a half a mile away—for if they'd been any closer they would know exactly how much coffee she drank every day.

Susan measured the ground coffee into the filter and Ruth poured the boiling water. As the water dripped through and collected in the coffeepot, Ruth beamed at her niece in satisfaction. "I must say, it's really nice to have you visit, dear. I'm only sorry it took such a disaster to get you out here again."

"Oh, Aunt Ruth, I'm sorry...I didn't mean to imply that with my tale of woe. That's why I didn't want to say anything on the way home from the station."

"I know, I know. You have no reason to be apologetic. Now let's just enjoy this coffee." She poured them each a cup, then continued. "As I was saying, Susan, there are two things we have to do. The first is to keep you occupied. Now—"

"But, Aunt Ruth—"

"No interruptions! At least listen to my ideas, all right?"

"Well, all right, but—"

"But you didn't come to clean out the turkey house, I know. What I have in mind, actually, is a different kind of activity. How long has it been since you spent a whole day working on a painting?" She watched her niece's face as she asked the question, and Susan's expression seemed to provide the answer she expected. "I thought so—far too long. And another thing: when was the last time you were on a horse?"

Susan smiled wryly into her aunt's kindly face. "Okay, you've made your point. From now on I'll trust you, and no arguments. Painting and riding...there's nothing I'd rather do!"

"Good. So the first part of the plan is easy. You'll go down to Lindesfarne first thing tomorrow morning and tell them you're going to stay for a

while. They'll be delighted to see you again, I know.
Marnie has asked me about you I don't know how—
many times, and Rafe always says the same thing:
'That Susan, such a good one with the horses.'
Champion is still at the stable, you know, and so is
Big Tiger."

"Big Chicken, we used to call him...remember,
Aunt Ruth? Hilary was out on him one day when
he startled a sparrow, and he nearly bolted, he was
so scared."

"Well, he is a bit of a chicken, I must admit....
Anyway, I'm sure you and Rafe will be able to come
to some agreement about finances. He can always
use an extra hand with the oats and the grooming."

"Oh, Aunt Ruth, that's a terrific idea! I can
almost smell the stables again, and hear those big
brutes whickering at the sound of oats being
poured into their buckets...." Susan, lost in her
reverie, was already hoping the next day would be
bright and warm. "Do you know, this is the first
time I've looked forward to tomorrow since...
since I got the news."

"I know, dear. Life isn't always easy. I remember
the day I parted ways with the young man who was
courting me just before I met Frank."

"What? You had another suitor? Aunt Ruth, you
are devious. All these years you've been holding out
on me!"

"Well, you didn't seem ready to hear this story
the last time you were here. You were still dreamy
eyed and full of happy-ever-after illusions...."

"I still am, I suppose. But tell me what happened.
What was his name?"

"Oh, his name was Peter, too, and he was something like your young man, now that I think of it.
He was pretty convinced that a woman should stay
home all day and cook. Not that that didn't appeal
to me, mind you, but—"

"But not when someone else is telling you to do it, right?"

"Well...yes," Ruth admitted. "I always _did_ like to speak my mind—and have things my own way, too, I suppose." She paused, brushing a stray wisp of hair from her eyes.

"So he wanted you to cook and clean all day," Susan prompted, sipping at her coffee.

"And I wanted to be a farmer. Oh, I was full of dreams in those days. I had the world all figured out, too. I was going to buy a little piece of land and a cow or two, some packets of pumpkin seeds from the dry goods store in town, and maybe a hen and a rooster. I was going to be an egg lady on the side..I had the house all built in my mind, right down to the chintz covering on the big armchair in front of the fireplace. And then...." Ruth sighed wistfully, her eyes behind her spectacles shining with a light Susan had often seen in the mirror in her own eyes, before she got that letter from Oxford.

"And then?" she prompted gently.

"And then I was foolish enough to tell Peter my plans." Ruth frowned, remembering. "It's not that he didn't like my taste in chintz, or that he wanted runner beans instead of pumpkins...."

"What did he say?"

"He didn't say anything at all, Susan—he just laughed. He laughed in my face. I was seventeen and more vulnerable than I would have believed. I was so shaken I couldn't even laugh back. I cried for a week and then...well, two things happened." Ruth took a sip of her coffee, set the cup on the table and leaned back in her chair. "First, I vowed I'd show that self-centered idiot that I wasn't someone to be laughed at. I would become a lady farmer, even if it was the last thing I did!" Ruth's voice shook with remembered emotion.

Susan pictured Grasshopper Hill in her mind's

eye. Everything was neat, tidy, and prosperous looking. "Well, you succeeded, Aunt Ruth, even if you wound up with turkeys instead of cows. Did your Peter ever see Grasshopper Hill?"

"Oh, I made sure he did, believe me! I dragged him out here one day by the scruff of the neck and made him walk over every inch of land I owned. I bet he had sore feet for weeks! But I didn't care, I was so proud that I'd done it."

The two women sat quietly for a few moments, contemplating the vagaries of the human heart. Finally Susan spoke.

"You said two things happened. What was the other one?"

"The second thing happened shortly after I'd paid off my last loan and given Peter the grand tour. At the time I had cows, horses and quite a few crops. I was having a hard time keeping up with the work—"

Susan's laughter interrupted the narrative. "You? Too much work? I'll believe anything else first!"

The older woman smiled at her niece's teasing, then continued. "Well, as impossible as it may sound now, it was true. And one day, one hot, sunny summer day as I was carrying what seemed to be the millionth bucket of water out to my thirsty kitchen garden, a persnickety young man in a fancy hat leaned over the gate, looked me right in the eye and said, 'Turkeys.'"

Susan looked at her aunt dubiously. "Turkeys?"

"That's just what I said at the time. I looked at his hat, at his shiny shoes, and at the trousers with the razor crease, and I said, 'Turkeys?' 'That's right,' he said. 'Unless you want thousands of dumb chickens running in and out of your kitchen all the time.'"

"Chickens?" Susan asked her aunt.

"'Chickens, turkeys, who cares?' this persnickety chap said. I must admit I thought he was a bit crazy, but it was a nice day, and I needed a break, so I set down my bucket and opened the gate. In he walked, as if he owned the place, and sat down in a lawn chair beside me and lighted a cigar. I watched him smoke for a minute and then I got up and started for the bucket—I never could relax for too long. But before I took three steps he was at it again. 'Yes, turkeys,' he said.

"'Turkeys! Chickens! What is this nonsense? I have to get to work!'

"'Well, all right, ma'am, but while you're filling that bucket, and carrying it, and emptying it, and filling it again, just think how nice it would be if all those cucumbers were turkeys. You don't have to water turkeys, you know, weed them, or plow them, or pick them. And if you're worried about how much work it takes to sit here in the garden with a pan of grain on your lap and feed them, you just set your mind at rest—I'll do it for you!'

"And that, my dear, is how I met your uncle."

"Aunt Ruth, are you serious? Uncle Frank said *that*?"

"He certainly did! And I ask you, what girl could resist such a proposal? Before I knew it I was married...and the proud owner of seventy-two turkeys."

Susan laughed as she got to her feet and picked up both coffee cups. "Well, I must say it's one of the most romantic courtships I've ever heard about," she said. "And now I think those dishes have probably soaked themselves clean."

"If you wash, I'll dry," Ruth offered.

"I'll go for that," Susan said, knowing that Ruth's idea of drying dishes meant leaving them in the draining board for the evening. Still smiling over the story of her aunt's engagement, Susan rolled up her sleeves and plunged her hands into the soapy water.

Chapter 4

Twenty minutes later the draining board was nearly full; only the spaghetti pot remained floating in the sink. Susan made a few halfhearted passes at the pot with the dishcloth, then straightened, a thoughtful look on her face.

She glanced over at her aunt who was sitting at the kitchen table looking through some catalogs. Then she turned back to the spaghetti pot and scrubbed away at it for a while. When she looked up again it was to find Ruth staring at her.

"Susan, dear, you needn't try to scour your way right through that thing."

Susan looked at the pot. It was sparkling clean. She rinsed it and balanced it precariously on top of the other dishes.

"I don't think that pot's been that clean since the day I bought it," Ruth commented, putting down the catalog she'd been holding. "I hope nothing's wrong. You seem a bit preoccupied."

"Well, to tell you the truth, there is something I was wondering about...."

"Sit down and tell me about it," Ruth invited. Susan joined her aunt again at the old wooden table. "Now what's the problem?"

"Well, I'm still waiting to hear about the other attack you mentioned."

"Attack?" Ruth looked at Susan questioningly, her hands playing with the pencil she'd been using.

"That's what you said: 'attack on two fronts,' as I recall."

Ruth blushed and set her fork down. "I suppose I did, didn't I? Well, Susan, you're going to have to forgive an older woman's fancies just this once, okay?"

"What do you mean, forgive your fancies? I know you, Aunt Ruth...you must be hatching some devious scheme! You are, aren't you?" She caught a glimpse of the sparkle in her aunt's eyes. "Something so devious you don't even want to tell me about it!" She was about to continue but her aunt's laughter interrupted her.

"You're right as usual, darling, but I'm afraid you're not going to win me over and make me tell you about it this time. This is my secret, and you can ask me all the questions you want—I won't say another word about the little plot I'm hatching." As if to prove she meant it, Ruth picked up her catalog again and opened it—upside down.

Susan laughed at her aunt's antics. "All right, you win. But I'm warning you, Aunt Ruth, if your nefarious scheme backfires, I won't be able to help you extricate yourself—especially if I don't know what it is. You'll have no one but yourself to blame."

Ruth mumbled something, her nose buried in her catalog.

"What did you say, Aunt Ruth?" I couldn't hear a word of it."

"I said it won't backfire, so don't worry, young lady. And now, if you don't mind, I have to get back to those horrible accounts I'm working on. They're the only part of my job I don't like, so I guess I can't really complain.... But I'd like to meet the idiot who invented ledgers in the first place. I'd give him a piece of my mind!"

Ruth got up and headed for the little room she'd converted into an office, whistling under her breath.

Susan finished wiping off the counters and went upstairs. After everything she'd been through that day, she was totally exhausted. *The train ride didn't help*, she thought as she changed into her nightgown. *By tomorrow I'll be feeling more energetic.* She folded her clothes neatly and climbed into bed with one of the novels she'd brought with her. After glancing at a page or two, she set the book down on the night table and turned out the light.

Damn Peter anyway, she thought as she sought a more comfortable position in the huge old bed. *I hope I taught him a thing or two—I hope he's feeling miserable!* She grinned mischievously at the thought that she might have knocked some of the stuffing out of his impeccably tailored shirt. Feeling a little happier she turned on her side and fell into a dreamless sleep.

IT SOUNDED LIKE there were a million sparrows on her windowsill when Susan woke up. She lay still for a few minutes, trying to figure out why there were so many sparrows in London all of a sudden, and why there wasn't any noise of traffic yet. Then she stretched luxuriously, her eyes closed. *If it's the middle of the night, that would account for the lack of traffic*, she thought, wriggling her toes, *but whoever heard of sparrows singing in the dark?*

She opened her eyes and raised her head from the pillow. Sure enough, there were a lot of sparrows on her windowsill, all of them twittering busily. And she was in Hampshire, not London! As she became more fully awake, she heard the kettle whistling downstairs and the sounds of Aunt Ruth puttering around in the kitchen.

"Hampshire," Susan said out loud, feeling a thrill of excitement. She jumped out of bed and went to the window, whistling back at the sparrows, who twisted their little heads as they eyed her curiously.

"Boo!" she said to them finally, and then dressed hurriedly, anxious to see what this bright, sunny day would bring. She felt like a teenager again, looking forward to the day with an avid curiosity untainted by the sophistication she was familiar with in London. As she pulled on her sweater she remembered the plans she and Aunt Ruth had made the evening before. This morning she would go to Lindesfarne and renew her acquaintance with Champion and Big Tiger. She pulled on her boots and ran down the stairs.

"Well, that's more like it I must say," Ruth said as Susan entered the kitchen and gave her aunt an exuberant hug. "You haven't run down the stairs like that since you were about twelve and ready to poke your nose into any trouble you could find."

"I feel like I'm twelve again . . . well, maybe four-teen," Susan said, an impish grin on her face. "What's for breakfast? And is that old brown bicycle still around—the one Hilary and I used to fight over all the time? I thought I'd ride it over to Lindesfarne after breakfast."

"It's here somewhere, I think. . . . At least, I don't remember donating it to any of the local garage sales. You might have a look in the barn. And if it's not there, you can try the garage. I'm sure both tires are flat. Why don't you pump them up while I cook us some bacon and eggs? The tire pump is on the shelf in the garage—at least, that's the last place I remember seeing it."

"Thanks, Aunt Ruth," Susan said, heading for the door. "I'll be back in ten minutes." She ran across the grass, which was still wet with dew, and went into the garage where it took her eyes a few minutes to adjust to the darkness. Then, as she looked around her, years and years of summer memories came crowding back into her mind. The wagon she and Hilary had used to collect eggs in was collecting dust in one corner; six or seven homemade bows and arrows hung from a hook on the wall. Her old fishing pole was lying under the window, as was Hilary's miniature windmill, which she'd invented one hot afternoon after lugging water out to the kitchen garden. Standing forlornly behind the door, both tires flat and its chain rusty, was the old brown bicycle. At one time it had been a three-speed, but it had been stuck in second gear ever since Susan could remember. She and Hilary had called it a two-speed—one speed uphill and one speed down.

She poked around on the shelf until she found the tire pump and a can of oil. Then she pushed the bicycle out into the sunshine and got to work with the pump, hoping that there were no holes in the inner tubes.

She had just started on the second tire when Ruth called her in for breakfast. The smell of frying bacon came wafting out onto the lawn as the door opened, and Susan dropped the pump immediately and went inside.

"Smells good, Aunt Ruth! Want some help?"

"No, everything's all ready. I just have to pour the tea."

"Look at all this food!" Susan exclaimed as she sat down at the table. "Mom tried to get me to eat like this in London, but somehow I never had the appetite. This morning, however, I'm starving!"

"Well, eat up, dear. There's plenty, and we can always make more."

"This is lovely! Homemade jam, fresh bread...and

these eggs are huge! I'd almost forgotten how much more delicious everything tastes when you're really hungry."

Ruth looked at her niece affectionately. "You're not regretting your impulsive decision to visit your old aunt, then?"

"Are you joking? I'm going to ride and paint all day—and probably gain ten pounds a week."

"You will if you keep eating like this.... Want some more toast?"

"How can I refuse? But I'll get it—you finish your tea." She sliced two pieces of bread and dropped them in the toaster. "Is there anything I can do for you before I go to the stables?"

"No, I don't think so, love. I'm going to be in Farnham all morning, anyway. Young Alec at Wilf's Garage is going to have a look at the Mini, and I'm planning to browse around the shops while he gives it a tune-up."

"Well, if you think of anything in the next few minutes, let me know," Susan said as she buttered the toast.

"You just relax today, dear, and have a nice ride. Take a holiday for a few days, before you start worrying about what has to be done. I'll always tell you when I need help, you know."

"Yes, I seem to recall—"

"Now, don't you start, Susan Baker!" Ruth said, laughing at her niece's teasing.

"All right, I'll stop, I promise," Susan said. Swallowing the last of her toast, she cleared the dishes from the table and helped put away the food. "Well, back to the old tire pump," she said, as she headed for the door. Ten minutes later she stuck her head in the door to tell her aunt she was leaving. Then she climbed on the old bike and, wobbling slightly, headed down the driveway.

Lindesfarne Stables was only a mile from Grasshopper Hill, and Susan coasted most of the way there. The road was a little bumpy, but safe enough if she watched for potholes. She could smell the clover as she pedaled along. The birds were singing, the flowers were blooming, the stream was bubbling over the pebbles in its path—the whole world was beautiful. *Why did I ever want to live in London,* Susan wondered as she coasted down a small hill. *Even Oxford could never match this.* She slowed the bike down, rode a few feet into a field and stopped, still straddling the seat. Breathing deeply of the country air, she looked around enthusiastically, noticing a thousand different pictures she could paint. Not could—*would,* she promised herself, and started pedaling again.

A few minutes later she was dismounting in front of the stables. She propped her bike against the stable door and wandered into the huge, musty building. The whinnying of several horses greeted her approach, and a man came toward her from the back of the long room.

Susan couldn't see very well in the dim light. "Rafe?" she asked uncertainly. "It's me...Susan."

"Susan? Susan Baker?" Susan's eyes had adjusted to the light, and she recognized the white hair and mustache of old Rafe. "Well, well, my dear, it's been a long time. You've grown into a very lovely lady!"

"Thank you, Rafe! You're not looking bad yourself. How's Marnie doing? It's been much too long since I was here last."

"You're right about that, Susan. Come on into the house with you, and we'll have a spot of tea with her. We can catch up on old times."

They moved toward the door of the stable. As they passed one of the stalls, there was a sudden commotion—a loud whinnying accompanied by the sound of a shod hoof beating against the old wooden floor. A magnificent chestnut head appeared at the door to the stall, and Susan cried out in delight. "The Champion!" she said, going over to the stall. The chestnut lowered her head, butting Susan's shoulder affectionately.

"The old girl still remembers you," Rafe said as he watched the mare's antics. "Well, come on, lass, let's have our tea and then there'll be plenty of time to renew your friendship with Champion." Rafe put his hand on Susan's shoulder as they moved to the door.

They were only a few steps from the house when the kitchen door flew open and Marnie ran out onto the step, throwing her arms around Susan in an exuberant welcome. "Susan Baker! My goodness, how nice to see you again!" Laughing and talking at the same time, Marnie held Susan at arms' length as she took a long look at the visitor. "But you're looking fine in spite of all that London living," the older woman commented impulsively. "Come on in! Have some tea and tell us what you've been doing with yourself all these years."

Chattering excitedly, Marnie led the way into the huge, sunny kitchen. The kettle was just boiling, and Rafe and Susan sat down at the gleaming wooden table as Marnie bustled around making a pot of tea and slicing some wonderful-looking seed cake onto a platter.

"No doubt Ruth fed you a huge breakfast, but here's a bite to eat anyway—you must be hungry after that bike ride," Marnie said as she set the teapot and the platter in front of her guest.

"Even though it's downhill almost all the way here," Rafe teased as he helped himself to a slice of cake. "Now that you're here, though, don't you think you should trade that bicycle for a horse?"

"I'd love to," Susan answered. "As a matter of fact, I was hoping we could come to some sort of arrangement for a while. I thought maybe I could do some work for you in exchange for horseback-riding privileges."

Rafe smiled. "Sounds like a good plan to me. How about if you take care of whoever you go out riding on? Muck, rubdown, feed and water...is that fair?"

"More than fair," Susan exclaimed, reaching for another slice of cake. "When can I start?"

"Champion's ready for a ride as soon as you finish your tea," Rafe replied, settling back in his chair. Marnie began plying Susan with questions about London and her family, and the three of them chatted for a half hour or so. Then Susan headed back to the stable, a happy glow in her blue eyes.

Chapter 5

Champion picked her way delicately among the trees and patches of bramble, stepping carefully over the rotting branches that were scattered on the ground. Apart from twittering of birds, the only other sounds were the jingle of the bridle, the creaking of saddle leather, and the occasional snorting of the big chestnut mare. Susan looked around contentedly. As she turned in the saddle all she could see was the forest—not a mark of civilization anywhere.

I've been living in London for too long, she chided herself. *I'd forgotten that any of this existed.* She reached into her knapsack and brought out one of the apples she had brought with her. She munched contentedly as Champion found her way out of the forest. Then, sliding out of the saddle, Susan fed a second apple to the horse. Champion stood patiently nibbling at the grass, as Susan stretched out lazily on the ground, the reins held loosely under one of her brown riding boots.

She remembered the day she'd bought those boots. "The last pair you'll have to buy," her mother had said, "now that you've grown the feet of a woman." Susan had been fifteen and very self-conscious. Her mother's words had made her feel proud and mature. She had bought the boots in London in the spring, just before the last summer she had spent in Farnham. Ever since then they had lain carefully in a box in her closet at home, but twice a year Susan had taken them out of their box and lovingly cleaned and polished them.

Mr. Baker had caught her at it one Sunday afternoon, as he'd come upstairs searching for the family's big atlas, *The Times* Sunday crossword puzzle tucked under his arm. A sensible man, he had offered to treat his elder daughter to an afternoon horseback ride in Hyde Park.

Susan was a purist, however, and dreaded the thought of trying to recapture her country pleasures in the crowded city. She had explained her feelings to her father, who had laughed with her at the idea of trying to compete with the bevies of "high-fashion hoity-toities" who paraded like peacocks around the park every weekend. "Imagine if I tromped on a dowager duchess!" Susan had exclaimed, laughing.

"Or if your steed somehow acquired the habits of his canine compatriots," her father interjected, "and started chasing buses and taxis!"

"Or decided to get chummy with one of the policemen's horses!" Susan cut in. But her father had had the last word.

"The worst of all," he declared, tamping the tobacco down in his pipe, "would be if they rented you a lovesick stallion."

"Okay, dad, I'll bite. What would happen?"

"Well, you'd just get started on your ride and he'd take it into his head to go visit his girl friend. He'd hightail it across The Carriage Road, through the Corner, and right up to the beautiful bay mare

outside the gate at Buckingham Palace. Imagine!
Every tourist in London laughing and shouting
while your mount rubs noses with the Queen's
finest!" Susan and her father had had a fit of giggles
over Mr. Baker's improbable scenario, and Susan
had done an extra good job on her boot polishing
that year.

Champion neighed companionably, and with a
start Susan became aware of her surroundings
once again. Talking soothingly to the mare, she got
up, stretched and climbed once more into the
saddle.

She was in high spirits as she returned to Lindesfarne after a gallop across the fields. She returned
Champion to her stall, gave her a pailful of oats and
a pailful of water, and got busy with the curry
brush.

Forty-five minutes later, she waved goodbye to
Rafe and Marnie and climbed on the old bicycle to
pedal back to her aunt's cottage. She was feeling
exhilarated, and she realized with a feeling akin to
awe that she had even enjoyed mucking out
Champ's stall. *I must be going crazy*, she thought to
herself as she tackled the first hill. *This much happiness would drive anyone who wasn't used to it around the bend.*
She knew, however, that her mood was a fragile
one, balanced delicately on the sunshine, and she
wisely refrained from testing its limits. She turned
her attention instead to thoughts of the afternoon,
wondering if her aunt had anything planned for
her to do. She was determined to enjoy her sojourn
in the country, and she made a vow, as she pedaled
valiantly up the last hill, that she would let nothing
interfere with her carefully constructed peace of
mind. She would immediately smother thoughts of
London, Peter and Oxford as soon as she had them,
she decided.

Proud of her determination, she propped the

bike against the garage and entered the farmhouse humming.

THAT NIGHT Susan went to bed totally exhausted. She didn't know if it was the country air, her long morning ride or all the exercise she'd gotten that afternoon that made her so tired. Ruth's idea of a relaxing afternoon in Hampshire was enough to intimidate even the most stalwart, Susan had decided as she carried her eighth bucket of water out to the kitchen garden. She had been ready for supper, and was looking forward eagerly to a hot shower and bed, long before the sun was anywhere near the horizon.

But Ruth, her own energy unflagging, had kept her niece hard at work until six o'clock. They had enjoyed a pleasant supper together before Susan had headed upstairs, shaking her head at Ruth's intentions of going through some of her massive piles of paperwork. As she stretched out luxuriously under the handmade quilt on her bed, Susan vaguely heard her aunt moving around in her office. She closed her eyes, thinking eagerly of the next morning's ride and hoping for a bright, sunny day, and within two minutes she was asleep.

SUSAN HAD been at Grasshopper Hill for three weeks, when she woke up to a dull, overcast Saturday morning. Even though it was cloudy, the weather was warm and she wasn't deterred from going out on a morning's ride. Climbing into her jodhpurs and hastily buttoning her shirt, she went down to the kitchen where, as usual, her aunt was already moving around.

"You've been up for hours, I'll bet," Susan said, pouring them both some coffee.

"I'm at my best in the morning, I find," Ruth said, looking over the rim of her glasses, which were perched well down on the bridge of her nose. "You look like you had a good night's sleep. Are you still missing the honking of buses and taxis too much?"

Susan laughed as she poured fresh cream into her coffee. "Hardly! It's great to be here. And now that I'm no longer suffering the agonies of stiffness every morning after I ride, I'm not in the least put off by clouds or rain."

"Good girl," Ruth said, looking at her niece fondly. They chattered for a few minutes longer, then Susan got up. "See you at lunch," she said and was gone.

She rode for the better part of two hours before dismounting and allowing Champ to graze for a little while. With the reins held under one foot, Susan stretched out in the middle of a huge field, giving herself over to the sounds of early summer and the smells of pastureland. She thought dreamily of living like this forever.... Then she heard someone speak to her, and she gave a start. Sitting up, she found herself looking into the cool amused face of Lindy Barwick.

"Well, fancy meeting you here," Lindy said looking down at Susan from the back of a magnificent black gelding. "I'd heard you were at your aunt's and I had meant to visit...."

Was there a trace of hostility in the woman's voice, Susan wondered, or was it just the awkwardness of an unexpected meeting after so many years? "Hello, Lindy," she said, jumping up and dusting the grass from her shirt. "I've been here for a little over three weeks now, and I'm equally at fault. I've been meaning to look you up as well."

The tension persisted despite Susan's attempts to lighten the mood. As they rode back to the stables together, Susan told Lindy about her disappointment over Oxford and about her subsequent decision to return to the country and concentrate seriously on her painting.

Susan had unsaddled Champion and was beginning her chores when the other woman said, "Hilary mentioned you were seeing a lot of Peter Whitelaw. He was at school with my brother, did you know?"

"I knew that, Lindy, but I didn't think the two of them knew each other. Peter's quite a bit older than Anthony," Susan said, reaching for a shovel.

"Are you serious about him?"

"I'm...I'm not quite sure," Susan replied vaguely, once again taken aback by the coolness of Lindy's tone. *She's like an interrogator,* Susan thought. *She acts friendly enough, but I feel as though I'm being cross-examined.*

"You must come over for coffee sometime," Lindy commented absently as Susan, after checking Champion's water and bringing her some more oats, prepared to leave the stable.

"Thank you, Lindy, that would be nice," Susan murmured, aware of the insincerity of the invitation and of the subsequent likelihood that she would never take up the offer.

As Susan bicycled the mile back to Grasshopper Hill, she mulled over her strange meeting with Lindy Barwick.

"There was something definitely odd about her attitude," she remarked to her aunt a little while later when they were seated at the large kitchen table having coffee after lunch. "It was as if she really was interested in what I'd been doing, yet at the same time as if she couldn't have cared less."

"Well, I never liked her much, I must admit," Ruth said matter-of-factly. "She always was different somehow, even as a child. She was never quite as innocent or rambunctious as the rest of the gang that you and Hilary brought through here every summer, usually like a herd of wild horses."

Susan laughed. "We weren't that bad! And you

never complained. But about Lindy, there seemed
to be a purpose to all her questions. I felt like I was
on a witness stand, and I didn't want to give her any
information but at the same time I didn't know how
to parry her questions. And her eyes...."

"Put it out of your mind, love. If it suits you to
avoid her in future, then it should certainly be easy
enough to do so."

Susan got up and began to clear away the lunch
dishes, but Ruth put a hand on her arm. "I'll do
those, Sue. Can I ask you to do me a great favor?
Could you run into Farnham this afternoon and
collect a few things for me? I'm up to my eyebrows
in these damned accounts and I want to get them
done."

"With pleasure. What do you need?"

Ruth made out a list of groceries she needed, and
explained a few other errands. A short while later
Susan was scooting along in her aunt's Mini
toward Farnham.

It was a lovely old town, with many of the buildings constructed in the warm, mellow red brick
that was quarried locally. Though just outside the
so-called Stockbroker Belt—the wide ribbon of
wealthy commuter towns around London—
Farnham was prosperous, and many of its residents commuted daily to their jobs in London.

Farnham's an ideal place to live, Susan thought. *It's away
from the hysteria of London, yet close enough to it so that you can
drive in occasionally.* Farnham certainly had plenty to
offer its residents. There were a number of excellent
clothing shops and several good restaurants. Histori-
cally a market town like Cambridge, it still stood in
the center of rich, arable land, and much of the local
produce still found its way to the large outdoor
market where Susan was now headed.

Busy picking out fruit and vegetables from one
of the heavily laden stands, Susan didn't notice a

tall man approaching her through the press of people. At the sound of his voice she looked up suddenly.

"Richard Evans! How lovely to see you!" She found herself looking into a pair of good-looking green eyes. "Let me pay for these bananas—I'll just be a minute."

"Do you have time for a cup of tea?" he asked, taking her arm and leading her through the crowd to the street. "We have some catching up to do; it's been a long time!"

They walked a little way along the street to The Golden Apple Restaurant, where Richard ordered tea for both of them.

"You're looking well, Susan," Richard remarked, but the casualness of his comment was belied by the intense scrutiny of his gaze.

Susan felt suddenly self-conscious. Something about him had changed. He was older, of course, but not just in years. Forcing herself to look at him she tried to define the difference. What was it...? Certainly he was mature now; the attractive teenager she had played tennis with was now a strikingly good-looking man of twenty-four. His sandy hair, not yet bleached by the summer sun, made him look older, and his eyes, still the same startling green, now possessed a depth that she hadn't noticed before. His shoulders had broadened and he had filled out. In fact, he was now perfectly proportioned for his six-foot-plus frame. But there was something else....

"You used to be able to speak when I last saw you," he said with a grin, and Susan realized that she hadn't said a word for more than a minute.

"You've changed, Richard," she said artlessly.

"Do you care to qualify that remark?" he returned, eyebrows raised and a hint of teasing in his eyes.

"I'm not...sure I can. You seem somehow different from the fellow I used to ride with."

"I'm no longer someone to ride with, for one thing," he returned, his voice growing suddenly harsh. At Susan's startled look he went on, "Don't tell me you didn't notice my limp.... Isn't that the change you're referring to?"

"What limp?" Susan asked. "I wasn't aware... what happened?"

"I was thrown off my horse during a hunt a few months ago."

"Oh, dear!" Susan murmured. "But you're such a good rider! How did it happen?"

"The ground where we started off had a lot of rabbit holes in it," he explained in a flat voice. "I was keeping to a slow trot because of that fact, but one of the other riders in the hunt came up behind me and for some reason my horse bolted in surprise. Before I could steady her, she caught her hoof in one of the holes and we went for a tumble."

"How awful for you...! And a fool thing for the other person to have done! Anyone on a hunt should know enough to keep a good distance away from everyone else!"

Richard gave a dismissive wave of his hand. "The rub was that I was laid up in the hospital here with my leg in traction for three months."

"Are you still in pain?" Susan asked, her large blue eyes full of sympathy.

"Some days are more painful than others. I'm becoming a walking weather barometer. Now, what about you? You're just as beautiful as always. And you've changed, too, you know. You've grown up." Susan flushed under his searching eyes, feeling vulnerable at the turn the conversation had taken. Sensitive to her discomfort, Richard went on, "What brings you back to Hampshire? Don't tell me it's the pull of the soil and the rural life!"

"Perhaps that's exactly what it is," Susan replied, smiling back at him. "London's so noisy and dirty, and the tourists are going to be teeming in over the next few weeks. I thought I'd give it a miss for a while."

"I don't believe you."

"What?" she exclaimed.

"I know you better than that, Susan Baker!" he said bluntly. "I don't believe noise and tourists would drive you away from London. If it's something you'd rather not talk about, that's okay. But don't give me any nonsense about crowds!"

Susan just gazed at Richard, her eyes wide in surprise. He returned her look evenly, but his expression was gentle, as if he wanted to soften the impact of his words.

"For whatever reason you left London, Susan," he said softly, "I'm glad you're back."

Chapter 6

"Aunt Ruth!" Susan said breathlessly as she pushed open the kitchen door and set her packages down on the table. "I saw Richard Evans in town! We had tea together. Did you know he had the most ghastly riding accident?"

Ruth kept stirring the white sauce she was cooking as she turned toward her niece. "Yes, I knew," she answered. "It happened just after Christmas. There's still some local gossip about it, so I thought I'd let Richard tell you himself. I knew the two of you would run into each other eventually."

"I know you don't like to gossip," Susan said, surprised at her aunt's deliberate failure to mention something that she knew Susan would find of interest. "But what are the Farnham busybodies saying?"

"Well, dear, something about it not necessarily having been an accident. There were one or two witnesses.... Anyway, what I could have told you would have been a bit of fact and mostly speculation. And in this instance," she added, looking pointedly over her glasses at Susan, "I thought you'd be better hearing about it from Richard himself."

Knowing she wasn't going to get any more information out of her aunt, Susan let the subject drop, and the two of them continued with preparations for dinner. Throughout the meal, however, Susan's mind kept going back to her meeting with Richard.

"Richard's renovation business sounds very interesting," Ruth remarked, as if aware of her niece's thoughts. "A lot of the old oasthouses in these parts are being converted into very attractive homes. They're the buildings that used to house the kilns for drying the local hops, you know. Well, some of the architects are really good; they've kept the exteriors almost completely intact."

"Yes," Susan answered. "Richard was telling me a bit about it. He suggested that we go out tomorrow afternoon and have a look at one he's fixing up on the other side of Farnham."

"He's been pretty astute in catching on to the trend," Ruth went on. "When his parents died he'd been in the building business somewhere in East Anglia...Norfolk, I think. There were a number of cottages up there, I believe he told me, that he was modernizing—putting in heating and so on."

"He left Norfolk when his parents died?"

"Yes. It wasn't his own operation; he was working for an engineering firm up there. When his parents died he gave notice. He's gone back there a couple of times, he said, to have a look at the finished products and to talk to some of his former colleagues about starting up his own business here in Farnham. By all accounts he's doing very well, though he's only been at it for a little under two years."

THE FOLLOWING DAY Susan took her paint supplies outside to a particularly lovely part of her aunt's

property. The spot she chose overlooked a stream
that marked one of the boundaries of Grasshopper
Hill farm. The morning was clear and sunny and
Susan eagerly spread out the contents of her
satchel, including a Thermos of tea as her aunt had
suggested, on the ground.

For a long time she just sat there, admiring the
view and giving her mind over to the random
thoughts that tumbled through it. Even when her
attention turned to Richard and the surprisingly
strong emotional response she had felt at their
meeting the day before, Susan made no effort to
stem their flow. She had been startled, even
slightly dismayed, at her reaction to Richard.
Already, in one brief encounter, their relationship
had changed from a childhood camaraderie to
something subtler, deeper—something with an
underlying sensuality. More than once in the restaurant she had looked up to find Richard's eyes on
her, searching her face as if trying to read her
thoughts. He had looked at her as a man looks at a
woman.

Gradually, Susan brought herself back to the
present. The sun, she noticed, was sparkling on the
water and lighting up the daffodils in their bright,
yellow-capped glory. It was too beautiful a day not
to get to work! She set up her easel and opened a
tube of paint. The strokes seemed to fly from her
brush, transferring the panoramic scene into an
impressionistic pattern of greens, blues and yel-
lows on her paper. Susan had not done any painting
or sketching for a week or two, and as she worked
she could feel a deep contentment settle over her
like a mantle, the first real peace she'd experienced
for weeks.

It must have been at least an hour later when the
stillness was broken by the joyous barks of Willie,
Ruth's wolfhound. Susan looked up distractedly. A

tall figure was following the dog across the field, but she couldn't recognize who it was immediately in the glare of the sun. Then she noticed the slight limp, and with a flush of pleasure Susan waved a greeting to Richard.

"Wilhemina's brought a visitor," he said congenially, when he had come within earshot. "Do you mind if I've come early?"

"Not a bit," she began, then with a gasp shot one hand out to steady her easel, which was shaking precariously from the smack of Willie's tail.

"Ruth said you'd be around here somewhere," he continued, smiling at her. Then he turned to look at her painting. "It's lovely, Sue. Too bad you're not in the picture yourself; you're looking like a wood nymph today."

Susan looked down at her hands, feeling slightly confused. Was he teasing her, mocking the childishness of her tied-back hair and the smock she wore over her blue jeans?

"Sensitive thing, aren't you? You still can't receive a compliment graciously." There was warmth in his voice, however, and when Susan looked up, she saw that his eyes were smiling.

"Ruth has invited me to lunch, by the way. She said to tell you that it's ready, and that if we're not back in five minutes she won't wait. So shall we go?" When she nodded, Richard picked up her easel and folded it in one easy movement. When Susan had gathered up the rest of her things they began to walk slowly toward the house.

"Is it all right with you if we drive into Farnham right after lunch?" he asked. "I've had a meeting with one of my clients canceled, so I thought I'd like to go out to the oasthouse I'm working on earlier than we'd planned. I'll have more time this way to show you what we're doing to it. This one is particularly successful because of its location."

"That's fine with me, Richard!" she answered, still absurdly pleased at the prospect of being with him for a few hours.

"Great! I've already told Mrs. Norman, my secretary, where we'll be in case anything comes up on any of the other sites, but I don't think it will."

Lunch was a hilarious affair. Ruth regaled the two of them with stories about how she used to sing to the turkeys in the hopes of getting them to increase their egg output.

"Some of them I actually call by name; you get to know them individually after a while. And by Christmas—well, November, I guess—I'm usually sorry that I have to have them killed. Last year, I remember, there was a particularly fat capon called Harold. . . ."

Richard and Susan were still laughing as they drove into town after the meal, and Susan realized that already, after only a few weeks in the country, she was feeling more cheerful than she had in ages.

"There's magic in the air out here," Susan told Richard with a straight face. "I'll bet if we bottled it we'd make a fortune."

"My dear," Richard replied, turning on her a look of tremendous solemnity, "you are a genius. To think I've been working all these years fixing up houses when I could have been bottling air. We'll have to go into the business immediately."

They continued their game the rest of the way into Farnham, trying to outdo each other in coming up with outrageous names for the product. By the time they reached the work site they were both weak from laughing so hard.

"It's odd there aren't any workmen around here today," Richard remarked as he held the car door open for Susan. "Usually they don't go home until five-thirty or six o'clock."

He led the way to the front entrance of the

ancient building and proceeded to explain what changes he was making in converting it into a four-bedroom house. Already the carpenters had constructed the upper floor as well as a long graceful staircase leading to it, and they had also put up basic framework for the interior walls. The plumbers had come and gone, and the electrician was due to finish the wiring within a few days.

"From now on, the building will start resembling a home instead of a construction site," said Richard as he showed Susan around. "Come upstairs. I want you to see the view. It's quite fascinating seeing all of Farnham at once. And the countryside is truly beautiful at this time of year."

Steering Susan by the arm, he directed her up the flight of stairs to the second floor. As she climbed, her attention was focused upon a huge window above her. First she could see nothing through it but the blue and cloudless sky, but as she continued her ascent, the tops of trees appeared, and then the roofs of houses. As she neared the top of the stairs the view of Farnham was complete. Richard was right—it was beautiful. Green hills sloped down to the village and tall trees moved gently with the warm spring breeze.

Sometimes I feel like I really belong here, Susan thought. *I feel like this town is my home.*

Without moving, she gazed at the scene as if she were in a trance, unaware that time was passing. As she stood there, she felt a deep sense of peace pass over her. Finally a gentle touch on her arm reminded her that Richard had followed her up the stairs and was standing patiently on the step below her.

"Oh, I'm sorry," Susan stammered. "I'm blocking traffic. The view from this window is too wonderful for words! I could stand here all day and take it in. The designer must have had a stroke of genius to think of putting a window right here!"

Richard flushed slightly. "Well," he said after a
moment, "it seemed only logical to let in the glorious Hampshire sun—that is, whenever we have it.
Sometimes I dream of living in this house myself."

Susan turned to look at him. His eyes were shining with a pride she had never seen in him before.
His whole face seemed to be aglow, reflecting the
sunshine that was pouring through the huge window. Susan couldn't resist touching his shoulder
and saying "You're doing a fine job here, Richard.
You must be very pleased with your work."

Richard grinned. "Don't I know it! How many
people get paid for doing something they love to
do? It's a rare phenomenon these days. I'm a lucky
man."

Susan smiled. "Well, lucky man, shall we continue our tour? Do you want to do the honors and
lead the way?

"Are you kidding? It's ladies first on my construction sites. After you, Miss Baker!" he said
chivalrously.

Holding her nose in the air and pretending to
wear a long skirt in graceful imitation of an old-
fashioned dowager, Susan continued up the last
few steps to the second floor. As her full weight
came off the top step onto the landing, however, a
loud, splintering noise suddenly echoed throughout the shell of the deserted building. Before she
could so much as jump backward, the landing col-
lapsed beneath her weight.

With a scream she fell through the opening, and
a second later had landed with a thump on the
ground floor, where she lay crumpled and still.

Richard reached her in an instant, moving a piece
of broken board away so that he could see her face.
"Dear God!" he murmured. "Susan...!"

Her eyelids fluttered open and then closed again
with a grimace of pain.

"Don't try to move. Just take it easy," he said firmly. "I'm going to move a few more pieces of wood...there. Now, how do you feel?"

"Everything hurts," she said feebly. "But I think what's really the matter is my ankle." She tried to smile, but then closed her eyes again, her face white and her forehead wrinkled in a frown as if she were trying to stop from crying out.

"Can you move, do you think?" Richard asked her anxiously. "Don't do it quickly. I just want to find out whether I can move you or whether I should get a doctor here."

"I...I think so...."

A few minutes later they had managed to establish the fact that, apart from the shock and several lacerations, nothing really hurt or seemed injured except for her left ankle, which was already swelling quite a bit.

Confident that she wouldn't be injured further by being moved and anxious to get her to a doctor as quickly as possible, Richard lifted her carefully in his arms and carried her out to his car, where he set her gently in the backseat, her legs stretched out across his jacket.

"How do you feel?" he asked her as they were driving toward Farnham. "Pretty wretched, I should think."

In the rearview mirror, Susan's blue eyes looked black in contrast to the whiteness of her face. "What happened, Richard?"

"I *think* the beam supporting the landing must have given way," Richard said almost harshly. "I'm going to have the hide off of whoever's responsible...."

Susan weakly raised a hand in protest. "It was probably an accident," she said. "Just make sure it doesn't happen to anyone else."

"You could have fractured your skull, Susan! Don't you realize that?" Richard's knuckles were white as he gripped the steering wheel. Susan was too weary to argue or to even register much of what was going on. Her body felt battered, and she bit her lip as waves of pain washed over her.

Her eyes must have closed for some time, for she hardly remembered the trip to the emergency department of the local clinic. The faces of various members of the medical staff floated through her half-conscious mind, as did the realization that a doctor was doing something to her ankle and that eventually the pain was no longer so severe. The next thing she knew clearly was that they were driving slowly along the dirt lane to Grasshopper Hill. Richard was steering cautiously, trying to keep the ride smooth by avoiding as many of the ruts as possible. Finally he stopped the car and opened the back door to help her out.

Willie's welcome barking set a hammer pounding in Susan's head, and with a stifled groan she put her arms around Richard's neck.

"You'll be in bed in no time, Susie," he murmured into her ear as he carried her toward the house. "Just hang on for a minute or two longer."

"What in heaven's name—" Ruth began, as she saw the two of them. "Oh, my dear!" she gasped. "Susan...!"

Richard interrupted her. "Susan's had quite a fall. Her left ankle is badly sprained, but Dr. Dudding assured me there's nothing else the matter with her that being in bed for two days won't cure."

"Darling, are you all right?" Ruth asked. "Here, let me get the door...."

Susan opened her eyes and looked around. She was in her own bed at Grasshopper Farm. The reality was reassuring, despite the fact that her ankle was throbbing painfully. The doctor, she recalled, had diagnosed her ankle as having only been sprained, and after binding it with a tensor bandage and applying an antibiotic cream to her abrasions, he had given her some medication to take for her pain and had sent her home with Richard. Obediently Susan had taken the medicine and had gone straight to sleep, as that was all her exhausted body wanted to do anyway.

Dimly Susan could hear voices in the kitchen below, the muffled sound punctuated at one point by the shrill whistle of the kettle. She strained to hear what they were saying.

"Poor standards of workmanship these days, I say," she could hear Aunt Ruth saying.

"They're good men," Richard said, emphasizing his words as if he were repeating them. "We've never had anything like this happen before."

"What actually did happen?" Now Ruth was speaking in her businesslike tone of voice.

Richard must have lowered his voice, for Susan couldn't make out even a word of his explanation.

The discussion in the kitchen became a distant murmur, and the room began to blur in front of Susan's eyes as her thoughts started to wander. She tried to focus her eyes on the treetops visible through the window, but they, too, were becoming a blur as dusk settled into twilight. It was a beautiful time of day, she thought with a yawn. She would have to try to paint it sometime.

But then the voices downstairs grew suddenly louder and with a jolt Susan's attention was caught again by what they were saying.

"I simply can't believe that!" Ruth gasped.

"I can only tell you what I saw," Richard returned evenly. "I don't know who the intended victim was, but I do know what happened to Susan this afternoon was no accident. That board was sawed clear through."

Chapter 7

Susan's heart began hammering strongly and her head suddenly cleared. She lay perfectly still, trying to hear every word that was being spoken below. She was wide awake now, adrenalin pushing through her veins and sharpening all her senses. Not an accident...! Richard's words echoed in her ears and she was determined to hear more of the conversation downstairs.

"Tell me again, Richard, exactly what you saw." That was her aunt speaking, and Susan could hear the worry in her voice.

"In spite of your opinion about the quality of workmanship these days, the incident this afternoon was not caused by careless carpentry. The staircase and landing were both built properly. Why, my men moved some heavy equipment up those stairs only yesterday. I've been up and down them myself countless times. The landing was perfectly solid—that is, it was this morning. Somehow, since then, someone replaced the floorboard— it's a piece of thick plywood—with a similar-looking piece that was much thinner. Most of the supporting structure was untouched, except for the major joist that was sawed almost through. When Susan, even as light as she was, stood on the plywood, her weight took the whole landing down with her. The way it was fixed, that board could have supported scarcely twenty pounds!"

When Richard stopped speaking, the kitchen was so still for a moment that Susan could hear the china cups being set down on their saucers. Finally she heard Ruth clear her throat.

"So how could this have been done?" Ruth asked. "Weren't your men at the house today?"

"They should have been," Richard returned quietly. "Mike Wynn is the foreman. Remember him? He's the man who was in charge of the construction of Dr. Dudding's new greenhouse. You've said yourself that he's a reliable fellow. Well, for some reason, neither he nor any of the other men were there today when we arrived. I thought at the time that it was odd. They weren't there just now when I was looking over the site, either."

"Perhaps one of them had an accident as well," she suggested.

"I doubt it," Richard replied. "Don't forget, the landing was intact when Susan and I arrived. In any case, I'd have been the first to know about it, if there had been an accident. Furthermore, if for some reason all the men had decided to knock off for the day, they'd certainly have asked my permission."

"Why don't you give Mike Wynn a call?" Ruth suggested reasonably. "Find out what you can; there's probably a perfectly sensible explanation for all of this."

"I did that; he wasn't home yet. But I left a message with his wife for him to call me back. I'm going to go out to the site first thing tomorrow, of course, just before the men arrive."

"Keep me posted, Richard, will you?" Aunt Ruth asked. There was the scraping sound of chairs being pushed back from the table.

"By all means. I should be on my way. Tell Susan I'll drop by tomorrow to see her, would you? I'll probably have some time in the afternoon."

Ruth must have seen Richard to the door, because Susan didn't hear any further noise for a moment or two, until the clinking of china indicated that her aunt was carrying the teacups to the sink. That was the last sound Susan heard, for when Ruth looked in on her a few minutes later, she was sound asleep.

SUSAN OPENED her eyes the next morning just as her aunt put a steaming cup of tea down on her bedside table.

"How do you feel, darling?" The older woman asked solicitously. "Your color is certainly better."

"Still a little fragile, I must say," she replied, "but considerably better than last night. I felt as though someone had used me as a bowling ball! What time is it?"

"Nearly noon, love, but relax. You're not going anywhere."

"Thanks a lot for the tea," Susan replied, "and don't worry. I feel absolutely no inclination to move—for a little while at least. But I don't want you to have to fetch and carry for me. I couldn't bear to be a nuisance."

"Don't worry about it, love," her aunt smiled. "You'll never be a nuisance to me. Anyhow, it isn't as if I'm on my last legs yet!"

Susan looked at her aunt affectionately as she arranged freshly cut daisies in a vase on the dresser. Ruth certainly wasn't on her last legs! Susan knew she had more energy than many women half her age.

"What would you like for breakfast, Susie? I bet you're hungry after not eating anything since noon yesterday."

"Well...." Susan began, not wanting to put her aunt out.

"Of course you are! You just start on your tea and I'll be back in a minute, love."

Susan sipped the hot beverage for a few minutes, then lay back against the pillows. Her ankle was beginning to throb again, and the lacerations she had suffered were making her arms painful and tender. When Ruth brought up a fluffy omelet and two pieces of thick, homemade bread, she practically wolfed down the food, together with a second cup of tea.

Her meal finished, she put the tray on the bedside table and picked up the novel she was halfway through. But the romantic tale of a woman on the Cornish moors couldn't hold her attention for long, and after a few pages she succumbed to the sleep that was beckoning her.

When she woke again it was late afternoon, and Susan could hear voices in the kichen. Although the speakers were talking quietly it seemed to her that there was some kind of argument going on. Susan found herself straining in curiosity once again to make out the words. She recognized Richard's voice and heard him say something about a right to know. Right to know what, she wondered. Who had a right to know?

A minute or two later she heard Richard's foot on the stair—at least it was definitely a heavier step than her aunt's.

"So how's the invalid?" Richard asked with forced lightness as he walked into the room.

Susan smiled at him, but she noticed the look of concern on his face that he was making a valiant effort to hide. "Much improved, thank you, and thank you also for coming by."

His expression changed for a fleeting moment as he stood in the doorway looking at her, and Susan felt her cheeks color with the same self-consciousness she'd felt at the restaurant that day in Farnham when they'd met. To cover her shyness she said quickly, "You can come in you know, I'm not infectious!"

"On the contrary, I find you very infectious!" Richard declared with a wide grin, then covered the distance from the doorway to the dressing-table chair in a couple of long strides. "You're looking better, Susan, I'm happy to say."

"And no small thanks to the kind ministrations of my aunt," Susan supplied. "Richard," she went on after a moment, "it sounded like you and Aunt Ruth were arguing just now. What was it all about?"

He sighed and, with his back to the dressing table, stretched out his long legs in front of him before answering. The silence continued while he appeared to be collecting his thoughts. "I didn't want to tell you," he began, "but Ruth said you had a right to know...."

"Right to know what?" Susan prodded, mystified by his reticence. What was he trying to keep from her?

"Susan, your fall yesterday afternoon was not the result of faulty workmanship."

"I...I know," she confessed. "I overheard a little bit of what you were saying last night in the kitchen."

"Eavesdropping, eh?" But Richard's smile was teasing and there was no reproof in his voice. "You know then that your so-called accident was a consequence of outright vandalism?" Susan nodded, and he went on, "I spoke to Mike Wynn, the site foreman, last night. Naturally enough I was anxious to get to the bottom of this."

"Go on," Susan prompted as Richard paused again.

"I asked him why none of the men were on site yesterday when we got there...and he told me that I myself had given them permission to leave."

"What?" Susan asked in surprise.

Ignoring Susan's interruption, Richard continued. "Naturally Mike was a little puzzled himself when I questioned him about the situation. After all, he thought the permission had come from me." He laughed humorlessly, then put up a hand to stop Susan from saying anything. "It seems that Andy Norman, my secretary's young son, had bicycled out to the site with a note asking Mike and the men to meet me at The King's Arms at noon to discuss some new designs for another house I'm starting to work on. Of course, they followed the instructions and took off for the pub. They waited there for me for an hour or so, and by the time they decided I wasn't going to show up, they had consumed sufficient quantities of beer for Mike to reckon he'd better give them the rest of the afternoon off. He said none of them were in a fit state to go back to the site and accomplish a reasonable amount of work."

Susan looked at Richard in dismay. "Was your signature forged on the note? Didn't they recognize that it wasn't your handwriting?"

"It was typed, but I apparently initialed it. Mike showed me the note this morning; my initials were printed. Anyone could have done it."

"But why, Richard? What's going on? Who would want to hurt anyone on your construction site?"

"I have no idea!" Richard rejoined. "People around here carry grudges, Sue, you know that. But I can't think of anyone I may have unwittingly antagonized."

Susan thought for a moment. "Nobody that's jealous of your success? Or that you've crossed in love?" She added teasingly.

For a moment a frown passed over Richard's face. Susan had the distinct feeling that something she had said had struck home. But then he shook his head. "Not that would merit setting that kind of death trap! You were really, really lucky to end up with just a sprain."

"Don't I know it! Thank heavens my own life is so uncomplicated. It's been virtually free of any confrontation ever since I got here, I'm pleased to say."

"You mean it wasn't before?" Richard probed gently.

"Well, I had a bit of grief before I left London, that's all," Susan said hastily, still unwilling to tell Richard about her quarrel with Peter and her disappointment over not being accepted at Oxford.

"Ah, yes, the noise and the tourists," he teased. Then, noticing Susan's discomfort at his jibe, he deftly returned to the question immediately facing them. "Well, I'm glad you haven't found any grief here yet, except for this horrible accident. I must say, that's the last time I'll have a woman precede me around a construction site. You're the last person I would want hurt...."

"And probably the quickest to heal. My ankle hurts like crazy sometimes but it's already getting better. Remember the summer I broke my arm falling out of Rafe's apple tree? I was hardly in a cast before I was out of it again."

"Healthy and attractive," Richard concurred. "Even in your blue pajamas. You're a good-looking woman, Susan, and you're going to have to learn to take it in your stride. Want me to try to convince you of it, now that you can't get away?"

"You wouldn't dare!" Susan protested, feeling the telltale color flood her cheeks again.

"Don't count on it. But, my sweet, I must go. Look after yourself." Richard brushed her hair with his lips and was gone.

IN LESS than a fortnight Susan was on her feet again. The cuts on her arms had healed almost completely, leaving only a wide band of yellow bruising in their wake. Her ankle was still hurting her slightly when she stood on it too long, but basically everything was back to normal. She was more than delighted to be getting out again, for the long days in bed had become tedious to someone as active as Susan.

Dr. Dudding, who had been keeping an eye on her progress, had dropped in every few days to check up on her. After examining her ankle he usually stopped in the kitchen for a cup of tea with Ruth, and Susan began to suspect that he was less interested in his patient's health than he was in her aunt's company.

He was a typical country doctor, Susan thought, complete with a Harris-tweed jacket that had seen better days and a black medical bag that looked so worn it surely must have been the same one he'd started out with thirty-odd years ago.

He seemed like a gentle man, with warm, twinkling brown eyes and a thick head of gray brown hair that kept falling in his eyes. He was fit as a fiddle and thought nothing of taking ten-mile constitutionals with his dog. Fad-crazy was how he described the joggers in their fashionable sweat suits whom he saw running along the roads and lanes. "Wonder if they'll keep it up when the trend changes?" Susan remembered him saying with a snort.

Dr. Dudding had finally told her she could ride again, provided she kept her mount to a gentle pace and someone helped her into the saddle. Under no circumstances, he explained, must her left foot take all her weight, as it would do if she mounted unassisted. Since she had been given the green light, she had twice been out for a ride on Champion, and it was to Lindesfarne now that she was headed.

Even for the middle of May, the morning sun was already hot as Susan drove Aunt Ruth's Mini the mile to the stables. She missed riding the old brown bike, but she knew her ankle would never take the punishment of pedaling back uphill to the Coleman farm.

When Susan arrived at Lindesfarne, she spotted Rafe mucking out one of the stalls at the far end of the stable. "Morning, Rafe!" she called.

"Hello, Susan, how are you today?" he called back, leaning his shovel against the wall. Marnie had called Aunt Ruth a few days after the accident to ask after Susan, since she hadn't been around. They had been sorry to hear about her accident, and Rafe, the first day she had come riding again, had said with a twinkle in his eyes, "We'll have to be a little more careful around construction sites from now on, eh?"

With a straight face, Susan had agreed. She had refrained, however, from repeating Richard's suspicion that the damage to the staircase in the old building had been willful. Now she walked into the barn, still putting her weight gingerly on her left foot, and asked the farmer if Champion was available for some exercise. "Still nothing too strenuous, Rafe; doctor's orders!"

"Well, now, Susie, Champ's feeling a little poorly for some reason—a little under the weather, you might say."

"Oh? For how long?" Susan asked in concern.

"Just on to two days now, I reckon. Odd thing is, the vet can't make out what the problem is. Why don't you go over to her while I saddle up Big Tiger for you to ride?"

Susan moved down the row of stalls till she got to Champion's. The mare recognized her and nuzzled her velvety nose against Susan's hand, but she seemed listless and her coat had lost its shine. Susan spoke to the animal quietly, stroking her neck until Rafe called to say Big Tiger was ready. Rafe gave her a leg up and within a few minutes Susan was headed down the path that led from Lindesfarne to the first of a series of large, fallow pastures.

On either side of the path the fresh green grass rippled in the spring breeze that brought familiar farm smells to Susan's nostrils. It was a perfect day, clear and cloudless, and the steady rhythm of the horse's hooves lulled Susan into a blissful state of almost dreamlike serenity. The grass gave way to low bushes, as she steered Big Tiger past grazing cattle and thatched cottages toward an incline that marked the beginning of the first field.

From the top of the hill Susan got a magnificent view of the surrounding area: Lindesfarne at her back, Grasshopper Hill to her left, the outskirts of Bordon to her right. And before her stretched four long pastures. Behind those were several more fields containing hops that were long and green on their trellises.

She recalled what Richard had said to her a few days before her accident when the two of them had ridden to this very spot: "You know, Susan, some North Americans call their prairies God's country. But you know something else? Here—right here— is God's country to me. I love every square inch of this land."

Susan had looked at him, an almost strange sensation coming over her as she examined his proud, strong profile. They had stopped in silence, on the crest of the hill for several minutes, savoring the smells of the land and the tranquility of the countryside.

That had been an important day; it had been the first time Richard had been on a horse since his riding accident. The specialists who had examined him had told him that his leg had been so badly damaged that any further riding would likely be impossible. But suddenly he had made up his mind that he was going to ride again. Mounting the horse had been difficult for him, and Susan's heart had gone out to him as she'd watched his face crease in pain. But then old Rafe had come out to give him a leg up, and Richard had swing easily into the saddle. Once astride, he'd found that controlling his mount had not been as difficult as he'd anticipated. He didn't have much strength in one leg, which made guiding his horse awkward at times, but, because he had once been a highly skilled horseman, he soon learned to compensate with the sensitivity in his hands.

Their ride had been glorious, although by the end of it Richard had been quite tired. If he had been in pain, however, he hadn't mentioned it to Susan, though it seemed to her that his limp had been more pronounced as they left the stable.

As Susan cantered along, her thoughts jumped suddenly from Richard to Peter, and she wondered what mental somersault had made her think of him. Forcing her mind back to her ride with Richard, she played the mental game of trying to remember the way her thoughts had proceeded. Then she remembered what the connection had been. She and Peter had been walking in Piccadilly Circus in downtown London one Saturday night. Traffic had been at its most frenzied, and all the neon signs had been ablaze. With a sigh, Peter had told her how much he loved London, and how delighted he was to be there instead of in the small town in Shropshire where he'd been brought up. "Who needs anything more than this, Sue?" he had asked her. "As the saying goes, 'A man who's tired of London is tired of life.' For me, this is all I need."

For me, just as for Richard, this is God's country. There is more to life than London, Susan thought, feeling the sun on the back of her neck. *There's much, much more.* Not that she'd thought so then, of course. That was during the time she had thought that repudiating everything rural was the height of sophistication. *Well, I've changed my tune,* she thought to herself as, on impulse, she steered Big Tiger away from the entrance to the next field and into the adjacent wood.

The horse moved along steadily, scarcely breaking stride as it changed course. The underbrush grew prolifically until they entered the thick of the wood, and then the dense oak leaves blocked out the sun. Susan squinted as her eyes adjusted to the relative darkness, and soon she slowed her mount down to a walk, keeping one hand free to stop the lowest tree branches from swatting her face.

A little while later Susan became aware of the sound of another horse's hoofs on the path, and she looked back to find herself gazing into the ice-blue eyes of Lindy Barwick.

Chapter 8

"Hello, Lindy," Susan greeted her. "Nice day for a ride, isn't it?"

"I'd heard you had an accident," Lindy replied. "I'm surprised to see you riding so soon."

Susan was about to ask how Lindy had found out about her mishap, but then remembered Aunt Ruth's close friendship with Lucy Whilsmith.

"I really missed the exercise," Susan said with a smile, determined to be friendly. "This is my third time out."

Something about Lindy always put Susan on edge, and again she got the uneasy feeling, as she had on previous occasions, that each of Lindy's questions and comments had a purpose. *But she's always been a little strange,* Susan thought, renewing her determination to remain on friendly terms with the woman. "Dr. Dudding made me promise to take it easy, though, so I haven't put Big Tiger into a full gallop yet," she said. "I was just cantering across the field, and I must confess I found it exhilarating."

"Yes," Lindy agreed after a moment, "it's an

intoxicating feeling; a little like being drunk, you might say."

Susan didn't imagine the feeling to be at all the same, but she refrained from commenting.

"I'm ready to head back now," Lindy said suddenly. "I've got some things to do in town. Care to join me?"

"No, thanks, Lindy. But I'll start back toward the stables with you."

She turned back the way they had come and with her knees coaxed Big Tiger into a trot. Perhaps it was the sudden crackle of some small animal in the dead leaves, or perhaps some faraway explosion; whatever the cause, Big Tiger suddenly took off down the path at full gallop. Desperate just to hold on, Susan found it impossible to control the frightened animal. Branches slapped against her face, and at one point she could feel her hat fly off, loosening her hair so it whipped out behind her. In terror, she used every bit of strength her thighs possessed to grip the horse's sides and to keep her seat. Her ankle started to ache as she pressed it harder and harder against the horse, and the cuts on her face began to sting as they were further lacerated by pine needles and sharp twigs that hung low over the path.

At last the two of them came out of the wood and Big Tiger slowed down first to a canter, then finally to a walk. Sobbing with relief, Susan leaned over to stroke Big Tiger's neck. Once he was calm, she moved her hand to her face to probe the cuts she had received. By now all of her face felt numb, but she could feel the wetness of her tears; she hastily tried to brush them away as Lindesfarne came into view. Lindy, she knew, must have been left far behind by their mad dash through the forest.

"Looks like you've had quite a ride," Rafe said as horse and rider approached the stable. "Big Tiger's in quite a sweat." Then as Susan drew up beside him he noticed her face. Her eyes were closed, but tears were splashing unstemmed down her face.

"Susan, what the devil...here, let me help you down." He led the horse to the end of the stable, then reached up to help her dismount.

"I...don't think I can move." She was sobbing openly now. "My ankle...."

"That was quite a gallop, Susan. I thought the doctor told you not to overdo it."

Susan turned at the words, to see Lindy appraising her coolly. "Big Tiger seems to have a mind of his own," she replied, smiling weakly. "Perhaps the doctor should have had a word with the horse, as well."

"Your face is a sight; don't tell me you were out of control! Those cuts must hurt. I'll go get the first-aid kit for you." Before Susan could answer, Lindy had dismounted, handed the reins to Rafe, and marched off toward the tack room.

With what appeared to Susan as almost a sleight of hand, Rafe tied the reins that Lindy had handed to him to the fence, and then turned and reached up again to help Susan to dismount. She slid into the old man's arms, and when her left foot touched the ground, she cried out in pain.

"I'm...sorry to be a nuisance," Susan whispered. "I just don't know what got into Big Tiger. He...he took off like a whirlwind—I could hardly stay on. Thank God there weren't any jumps."

"Ssh, Susie, don't fret. Lindy's coming back with the first-aid kit now, and we'll have you right as rain in no time."

When Rafe had gently applied ointment and bandaids to her face, she looked around for Lindy, but the other girl was nowhere in sight. Susan was surprised she had left; she had wanted to talk to her more calmly about what had happened back there on the forest path.

"Just you go on home now, Susan, and don't give another thought to Big Tiger. I'll brush 'im down and feed 'im."

"Thanks, Rafe," Susan replied warmly. She was starting to feel calmer after the shock of the incident. "But I'd really like to have another look at Champ, to see if she's feeling better, and I could easily fill Big Tiger's pail full of oats while I'm at it." To stave off any protest from Rafe, she quickly hopped into the stable, away from Rafe's concerned gaze, and gingerly tested her left foot again. It hurt.

Nevertheless, she saw Champion, who was still looking as poorly as before, and managed to shovel a few oats into Big Tiger's pail before she finally settled herself in the Mini and headed homeward. Her ankle was throbbing painfully, and because pressing down on the clutch pedal was little short of agony, Susan contented herself with driving the mile back to Grasshopper Hill in second gear.

Once again looking like a battle victim, she hobbled into the farmhouse and gratefully accepted some brandy-laced tea as well as Ruth's loving ministrations—not to mention a stream of questions that she struggled to answer patiently and accurately. Susan was of two minds about whether or not to confide her suspicions to her aunt, but very soon Ruth's worried frown decided her.

"Lindy must have taken her crop to him, Aunt Ruth...I know it! There was nothing at all in the woods that could possibly have startled Big Tiger like that."

"But, Sue, you're the first to admit that that horse is the biggest coward on four hooves. You used to tell me he'd bolt at a sudden breeze."

"That's true," Susan agreed, trying to be fair. "He used to scare easily, but quite honestly he's

grown up a lot and seems much calmer than before.
And as I said, there was absolutely nothing to have
frightened him, that I could see, anyway."

"But surely if you'd just told Lindy that you were
under doctor's orders to take it easy...."

"That's what doesn't make sense," Susan said
heatedly. "Lindy's strange, perhaps, but no one
would deliberately hurt someone who's recuperat-
ing! It must have been an animal that scared Big
Tiger. But I must say, it sure felt like it was Lindy!"

"Susan," her aunt warned, gentle reproof in her
voice, "you've got no reason whatsoever to say
that. I agree that Lindy's not the easiest person to
be around, but that's not grounds for condemning
out of hand."

"I'm sorry. I know you're right," Susan confessed, contritely. "It's just that she seems to rub
me the wrong way these days...."

"I've told you before, Sue, if it suits you to avoid
her, it can be done. Why not try the stables on the
other side of Bordon? They're a little farther away,
but getting there takes only another few minutes
in the car. Now," Ruth went on briskly, "let's talk
about your appetite."

Susan was grateful to her aunt for trying to take
her mind off Lindy Barwick, but the memory of the
woman's cold blue eyes lingered long after Susan
declined the offer of lunch and hobbled upstairs to
lie down. Stretched out under the quilt, although
pushed to one side of the bed to accommodate the
spread-out form of the snoozing wolfhound, Susan
went over the morning's incident again, running
through the whole series of events in her mind's
eye. Why would Lindy have wanted Big Tiger to
bolt? Was Susan jumping to hasty conclusions
because the other woman was simply not as
friendly as another person might be? Lindy had
always been a little strange, but never sadistic....
Perhaps Big Tiger was nothing but a big chicken

after all. Maybe there had been a snake on the path, or a rabbit had suddenly scurried into its hole. A collage of bits and pieces of the incident came together in Susan's mind as the brandy-and-tea combination her aunt had given her began to numb her body and take her into the swirling vagueness of sleep.

It was after six o'clock when Susan awoke, disoriented and aching. Noticing that Willie had obviously finished napping and had left the room, Susan started to maneuver her legs into a more comfortable position. An arrow of pain shot through her ankle and she closed her eyes again to wait for it to ebb. She must try to get up, she told herself determinedly. If she put the tensor bandage back on her ankle again, she'd probably be fine—able enough, anyway, to be of some assistance with supper preparations. Dragging herself out of bed, she hopped over to her housecoat, which was lying on the chair beside the dresser. She was just headed out her door toward the bathroom when she heard a gruff voice coming up the stairway.

"Susan?" the voice boomed. "It sounds to me as if you're being foolish enough to walk on that foot."

Susan turned to see the tall figure of Dr. Dudding appear at the top of the stairs. "Hello, doctor! I didn't hear you come in. Willie usually announces visitors to the entire neighborhood."

"And your thoughtful aunt just informed me she put enough brandy in your tea to keep you sleeping soundly for hours—small wonder you didn't hear me come in!"

"Did...did Aunt Ruth tell you what happened?" Susan asked hesitantly.

"In a manner of speaking, yes. I'd like to hear your version, though. But first let's have a look at that foot."

Susan allowed the doctor to help her back to her bedroom, and she sat quietly while his gentle hands probed her ankle and around the cuts on her face.

"I'd like to clean these up properly, Sue, and then I'll bandage your ankle. You're certainly one to keep a fellow busy!"

Susan blushed at his teasing, feeling rather like a wayward child who had gotten into mischief once again. A few minutes later the two of them joined Ruth in the living room.

"I'll be quite confused having you back on your feet again, Susie," her aunt said, smiling at the bandages on her foot and face. "I'm getting rather used to you like this!"

"Would you believe me if I told you none of this was my own fault?" Susan asked, accepting the glass of sherry her aunt offered.

"Of course, love, you know I don't blame you."

The three of them chattered away comfortably for a little while, discussing everything from turkeys to politics.

Suddenly Willie sat up from the hearth in front of the fireplace and began to growl.

"I think we must have a visitor," Ruth remarked absently.

The doorbell rang right on cue as Ruth stood up, and with Willie bounding before her she went to answer the door.

"Evening, Ruth. Is Susan at home?"

Not recognizing the visitor's voice, Susan looked curiously toward the hall. A moment later the local vet, Dr. Fairweather, walked into the room.

"Evening, Susan, Stephen," he said, looking slightly embarrassed and shifting self-consciously from one foot to the other.

"Hello, Dr. Fairweather. You wanted to see me?"

"Yes, er, it's about Champion, Susan, at Lindesfarne. She died this afternoon."

"No!" Susan gasped, appalled. "I. . . I saw her earlier today, and she didn't look well, but—"

"No offense, Susan, but I'd really like to find out everything I can about what went on out there today."

"Dr. Fairweather, surely you're not accusing Susan—"

"I'm not accusing anyone, Ruth," the vet said steadily. "I'm only trying to find out what the old girl ate today, and what she ate over the past few days."

Susan sat wretchedly on the edge of her seat, twirling the stem of her sherry glass in agitation.

"What were the symptoms, Jake?" It was Dr. Dudding speaking, and Susan turned her large blue eyes, now opaque with worry, toward the vet, awaiting his answer.

"Listlessness, loss of sheen on the coat, eyes rolling back." Dr. Fairweather went through the symptoms like a checklist, all embarrassment gone now that he was talking as one professional to another. "Rafe had called me earlier on in the week when it was obvious the horse was sick. I gave her an injection, as well as some antibiotics in liquid form. Rafe was supposed to mix it in the feed once a day." The vet ran his hand through his thinning gray hair, then stroked his chin, still speculating on the cause of the horse's death. "They didn't seem to have any effect whatsoever," he continued wearily. "Rafe called again this afternoon to say Champion had started sweating heavily and was foaming at the mouth. She died only a few minutes after I got there."

"Have you ever seen symptoms like those before, Jake?" Ruth asked quietly.

"Decayed feed can cause approximately the same symptoms, but usually the horse recovers after vomiting. They sweat the same way, though, and often manifest the same listlessness. There was a case we studied once when I was a student in veterinary college. . . ."

Susan listened while the vet related the grisly details of a similar case, closing her eyes in a vain attempt to rid herself of the gruesome pictures her imagination was conjuring up.

"Well, Susan," Dr. Dudding questioned gently, "can you shed any light on this strange occurrence?"

"Just tell me everything you did with the horse over the last week," the vet prompted. "I won't bother you any longer than necessary."

Susan cast her mind back over the past week. "I...I ride Champ by choice...at least I used to," she began. "I usually saddle her myself, but this week, because of my ankle, Rafe's been helping me a little. Then at the end of the ride I always give her some oats and a pail of water."

"Did you ever stop in a field and let her graze?"

"Yes, once in a while. But I'm sure she only ate grass, Dr. Fairweather...I mean, I'm sure she never got hold of a dead animal or anything."

"Was it you who always fed her, Susan? Did you ever let one of the other riders do it instead?"

"Never!" Susan exclaimed. "Rafe and I have an agreement. He lets me ride for nothing, and in return I look after all the tack, feed the horse and occasionally muck out the stalls. It's a good deal, actually, and I wouldn't think of not keeping to my end of the bargain."

"Do you ride Big Tiger often?" the vet asked.

"I rode him today. Why?"

"It seems as though he's suffering from the same ailment."

"Oh, gosh," Susan murmured, and sat back wearily in her chair, "you must think—"

"I haven't any opinion so far, Susan," Dr. Fairweather said firmly. "I'm simply trying to sort out what's been fed to those two animals. Did you feed Big Tiger today?"

"Yes. He...he'd been rather frightened on the

ride, and I wanted to calm him down and take a last look at him before I left, to make sure he was all right."

"Well, thanks for your help, Susan; I won't take any more of your time. Good night, Ruth, Stephen." He walked toward the door and Dr. Dudding stood up in turn to see the vet out.

"He's going to do an autopsy," the doctor said as he reentered the room. "It seems that the illness has really got him stumped. He also asked me to pass on to you, Susan, his regrets about your mishap this afternoon. Rafe told him all about it, and I guess he was too embarrassed to refer to your battle scars while he was here."

"Thanks for passing that on, Dr. Dudding," Susan murmured, "though at this stage he must think me terribly incompetent."

"I shouldn't think he believes anything of the sort."

"Well, you must admit," Susan persisted, "the finger of blame does point in my direction, doesn't it? I mean, I'm really about the only one who rides at Lindesfarne—apart from Lindy Barwick. Gilly Evans is still at school, and Richard doesn't ride much these days.... And I was the one who fed them...both Champion and Big Tiger.

"Don't blame yourself, darling," Ruth said soothingly. "Dr. Fairweather wasn't accusing you. As Stephen says, he's probably just perplexed by this rather mysterious illness."

"I guess you're right," Susan agreed reluctantly. "All the same—"

"You're looking a little wan, love. Why not go on up to bed, and I'll bring you some supper on a tray as well as my special brew."

Susan realized that she was, in fact, very tired, and with a weary smile thanked her aunt for her kind offer. "No need to lace the brew this time, however," she said. "At the moment nothing hurts, and I really am exhausted. I know I won't have any trouble at all getting to sleep after supper." She kissed her aunt good-night and said goodbye to Dr. Dudding. Though still upset by the vet's news, she wasn't insensitive to the budding romance between her aunt and Dr. Dudding, and she was just as happy to be giving them a chance to have supper alone together.

Chapter 9

The next couple of weeks passed pleasantly for Susan. It was early June and the summer so far had been clear and sunny, with only the occasional cloudburst. In fact, some of the farmers in the area, Aunt Ruth had said, were complaining about the lack of rain.

"I still can't get used to the thought of someone complaining of drought in England!" Susan had exclaimed one beautiful day. She and her aunt had taken their lunch out into the garden, and both of them were seated comfortably in canvas chairs, soaking up the sun.

"You know that the weather is an Englishman's favorite topic of conversation," Ruth had remarked dryly. "What difference does it make if they complain about the rain or the sun?"

Susan had no answer to that, and addressed herself instead to the bowl of spinach salad resting on her lap. After she'd chased the last mushroom around her plate with her fork, she sighed contentedly and leaned back in the lawn chair, picking absently at a thread that had come loose from one of the seams of her pale green sundress. She turned lazily to look at her aunt, whom she found concentrating on the rose bush directly in front of her.

"They're lovely, Aunt Ruth," Susan said, following her aunt's gaze to the butter-yellow flowers. "They're more than that, they're heavenly."

"Yes, they are lovely this year," her aunt agreed with satisfaction. "They take a lot of work though. And on top of the gardening, there's the coop."

"What does the turkey coop have to do with anything?" Susan queried with a laugh.

"It needs painting, that's what."

"Madam, allow me. It's the least I can do after your valiant nursing job a few weeks ago."

"Never let it be said that an offer has to be made twice around this place," Ruth said emphatically. "Would you do it, Sue? It really would be a great help."

"Of course, Aunt Ruth, it'll be fun!"

AN HOUR LATER Susan was looking for a parking spot along the busy main street in Farnham. As luck would have it, she found a place directly outside the hardware store.

"Two gallons of paint suitable for a turkey coop, please," she said cheerily to the young lad behind the counter.

"Suitable for a what, ma'am?" the fellow asked, looking askance at Susan.

"A coop," she repeated. "A turkey coop."

"Oh," he said blankly, but was saved from demonstrating further ignorance by the arrival of the store's owner, Mr. Sheldon.

"Go help the other customers, Andy. I'll deal with the young lady." Clearly relieved, the young assistant walked away and began talking to a man about pliers.

"Do you mind my asking your assistant's name?" Susan asked the proprietor. "He...looks familiar."

"Why, that's young Andy Norman," Mr. Sheldon supplied. "You're Ruth Coleman's niece, aren't you?" At Susan's nod and look of surprise, he explained with a chuckle, "She's a regular customer of ours and she mentioned last time she was in that her niece was down from London for a visit. When I heard you mention turkeys, I thought to myself, 'I'll bet that's Mrs. Coleman's niece.' Pleased to meet you, Miss, er—"

"Baker... but please call me Susan."

"I certainly will. Morris Sheldon, at your service!"

"About Andy Norman, Mr. Sheldon...."

"Seems reasonable to me you might have bumped into him at some point. His mother works for that engineer who lives out near you."

"Richard Evans, yes, of course—I'm sure I must have met Andy before." Susan had her fingers crossed behind her back as she told this fib, but she was anxious to end the conversation for fear Mr. Sheldon might insist on "reintroducing" Andy Norman to her. For some inexplicable reason she didn't want to meet the lad face-to-face. The mystery of her fall in the oasthouse was still unsolved, but the memory of that painful mishap was still clear in her mind.

"Now, what color paint do you want, my dear?" Mr. Sheldon asked to Susan's relief, and together they walked from the counter over to the several rows of shelves that held various sizes of paint cans.

They settled on a dark green color, and Susan then purchased several more items such as a roller, brushes, and turpentine. As she carried it all out to her car in one armful, she tripped on the step outside the store, only to be caught by two strong arms.

"What, is the damsel in distress yet again?" It was Richard Evans's teasing voice.

Regaining her balance Susan gazed at him gratefully, flushing at his remark but refraining from
commenting except to thank him. Her sense of
mischief got the better of her, however, and she
added, "I guess you could say I have trouble standing on my own two feet...particularly where
you're concerned!"

"Well, that's quite a loaded statement; I wonder
what the lady means," he said mockingly, carrying
her bags to the car for her.

"I mean that you're always around when I need
you, it seems." Susan blushed again, realizing
almost immediately that her second comment was
even more provocative than the first. In an agony
of embarrassment she busied herself with re-
arranging the bags on the passenger seat.

"And may I be of any further service, pray?"
Richard went on mercilessly, obviously enjoying
the situation.

Susan turned to him, her cheeks still pink, and
said recklessly, "If you have a mind to paint a turkey coop, I'd certainly appreciate the help...."

Now what in heaven's name made me say that, she
thought as she drove back to Grasshopper Hill with
Richard following behind in his own car. *What was I
thinking of? He must surely have better things to do. I wonder
how I even had the nerve to suggest it? Especially after the little
exchange we had over my clumsiness.*

"You know perfectly well why you made the
suggestion," a little voice at the back of her mind
replied.

"It's not what you think," Susan said to the steering wheel, "he's just a friend."

Richard and Susan spent the remainder of the
afternoon laughing and painting, though it seemed
that, by the time they finally put down their
brushes, they had spent considerably more energy
on the former than on the latter. They called it

quits about seven, when Ruth came out to find them.

"Well, I'm ready for a gin and tonic. What about you two? After baths and clean clothes, of course," she added, eyeing the paint-spattered overalls of the two young people in front of her. "And there's a roast for tonight, Richard, that Susan and I could never finish by ourselves."

"If that's a dinner invitation, kind lady, I accept with pleasure and without hesitation," he said, gallantly bowing from the waist.

Richard headed to his car with a promise to return within the hour, and Susan, as she walked toward the kitchen door with her aunt, said, "I'll be down in ten minutes." Then she sprinted up the stairs to bathe and change.

"That young man certainly gave a helping hand," Ruth remarked as she and Susan scrubbed the potatoes and prepared the vegetables a little later.

"What do you mean, 'that young man'?" Susan demanded, turning to stare at her aunt. "You've known him for years; why so formal all of a sudden?"

"Perhaps I should call him '*your* young man.'" Ruth's eyes twinkled.

"Hardly!" Susan bent over her potatoes.

"He seems to be interested in you."

"Oh, he's just a friend."

"Well, I'd say he went beyond the call of friendship today. Anybody else would have left you and my foolish fowl without so much as a backward glance. Oh, don't think I didn't hear the squawks of the few odd birds that escaped!"

Susan looked sheepish. "I guess he feels badly about my accident.... He's the responsible type, you see."

"Yes, he's a good honest man—very fair, very kind and very intelligent." Ruth added some salt to the boiling water and threw a few potatoes into the pot. "He's very well thought of in these parts. More and more people are turning their building and reconstruction projects over to him. He'll do well financially—lots of the local girls would love to be affiliated with him."

Susan smiled at her aunt's delicate description. "Has he been 'affiliated' with anyone lately?"

"Oh, I believe he was involved with Marion McDonald for a while, and somebody mentioned that he's been seen on occasion with Lindy Barwick. There was talk of him and Jane Locke...I guess he's been around. Now I think he's rather taken with you."

Susan didn't know how to respond.

"There are lots of girls," her aunt went on, "who would give their eyeteeth to be in your position."

"Oh, Aunt Ruth, you're exaggerating."

"Not so! Many of the young chaps around town haven't got much in the way of brains or ambition. Just be careful, Susan. Some of the single girls may want to take him from you. Especially the ones who think they'll be old maids."

"I thought the term 'old maid' went out when women's lib came in."

"In a small town, a girl's prospects are limited. Most of the bright, ambitious young men go off to London, and when they move back here to buy a home, they have a wife and two children with them. The fellows remaining are, shall we say, not so eligible. Lucy Whilsmith's other niece, Lindy's cousin, Jennifer, decided to move to Manchester, since the only man in Farnham who was about her own age and still available—or so she claims—was Alec Stout. He's the young fellow who works part-time at the gas station in town. He's attending the local technical school."

"Oh, yes," Susan said. "If he's the one I think he

is, he's always making snide comments when I go to get gas. He's always saying I should go out with him but that I'm so stuck-up I'd probably never be seen with him."

"Well, go to another gas station, dear," her aunt said reasonably. "I only suggested that place because they service the car whenever it needs a tune-up, and I must say, they do a bang-up job. Anyway, Sue, I just thought you'd like to know that your 'young man' is much sought after around here!"

Susan refused to be baited by her aunt's repeated reference to Richard as her "young man," and instead made a face and offered to set the table.

"Thanks, love. Set it for four, would you? We're having another guest tonight."

"Oh? Who's the lucky person?"

"You'll see," her aunt replied calmly and couldn't be induced to say more.

A few minutes later Richard returned, and the three of them went into the garden to enjoy the warm summer evening. They sipped their drinks in quiet contentment, allowing the conversation to flow where it wanted to.

The calmness of the evening was broken a little later by the wolfhound's announcement of a visitor, and Susan went to the kitchen door. When she opened it, however, there was no one there. *Willie must be getting senile,* she thought with a giggle. She was about to shut the door when she noticed a long, green-papered package lying on the porch handrail. Flowers for the lady of the house, she wondered? Sure enough, beneath the wrapping lay a dozen long-stemmed white roses. Susan was about to open the small square envelope accompanying the flowers when the peal of the front doorbell echoed through the house. Still holding the unopened envelope, she went to the front door,

this time hoping there would be someone on the
other side.

"Dr. Dudding!" Susan exclaimed with pleasure.
"A social call, I hope?"

The attractive doctor walked into the hall, nodding in answer to Susan's question. "Better not
open that," he said gruffly, indicating the envelope
in her hand. "It's for your aunt—" turning red as he
suddenly realized he'd given away his little game.
Susan tactfully turned back toward the kitchen,
hiding her smile and stifling the giggle that was
forcing its way to her lips.

"The flowers are lovely, doctor. Aunt Ruth will
be thrilled." *There's romance in the air*, Susan thought
with glee. *I can smell it as easily as I can smell the roses.*
When she was sure the doctor had gone out to the
garden and was well out of earshot, she succumbed
to a gurgle of laughter at the thought of the gruff
Dr. Dudding depositing the flowers on the back
step and then charging around to the front of the
house, attempting unsuccessfully to look the picture of innocence.

The evening turned out to be quite festive.
Richard had brought over a couple of bottles of
excellent Burgundy, and Ruth made Irish coffee to
finish off the superb meal. Everyone was in high
spirits, teasing each other and laughing. The flowers from the garden were offering their heady fra-
grances as a complement to the balmy night air,
and after dinner the two couples moved outdoors
again with their coffee to savor the last of the
evening.

When Susan finally crawled into bed, she
thought again of how radiant her aunt had looked.
The sparkle that had been in her eyes when her
husband had been alive seemed to have been
rekindled. Dr. Dudding had thoroughly enjoyed
himself, Susan knew, and it had only been Ruth's

threats to leave him in the garden alone for the rest of the night that had finally induced him to take his leave.

And then there had been Richard.... He had been utterly charming all evening. Susan had noticed how he had frequently offered to help Aunt Ruth with various plans she mentioned, and how easily and knowledgeably he spoke on a wide variety of subjects. And to Susan he'd been very attentive, asking her perceptive questions about her art and her ambitions concerning it. Yet, tactfully, he'd refrained from probing into her reasons for leaving her job in London and returning to the country. To Peter Whitelaw, he had made not one reference.

There had been almost a magic in the air that night, Susan thought. The wine, the aromatic garden, the gentle evening breeze—whatever the cause or causes, something had stirred in her. She had been electrifyingly sensitive to Richard's nearness all evening, and more than once she'd turned to find his sea-green eyes gazing at her intently, unwavering in their examination of her. But she hadn't felt self-conscious as she had in the past. She had returned his looks, her large eyes drinking in his finely molded features and the proudness of his profile. She had seen him to the front door after he'd said his goodbyes to her aunt and Dr. Dudding. He had looked at her for a long minute, then had taken her in his arms. To Susan it had been the most natural thing in the world, the logical and fitting culmination to the evening. At first he had kissed her gently, but imperceptibly his kiss became hard, passionate and probing. It had demanded a response from her and she'd given it freely, winding her arms around his neck to draw him closer. Her body had been ignited by a passion that had surprised and thrilled her, and when

Richard finally pulled away, she had felt empty and unsatisfied. When he left, she'd stood a long time at the open door staring down the driveway, trying to control the turbulent emotions coursing through her before returning to her aunt and the doctor and bidding them good-night.

"IT WAS a super evening, Aunt Ruth," Susan told her aunt as she came down to breakfast the next morning. "I can't remember when I've enjoyed myself so much."

"I agree, darling. There's a bloom in your cheeks this morning, and I don't think, somehow, the abundance of wine is the cause."

Susan blushed and turned to put the kettle on. "You're looking pretty starry-eyed yourself," she returned mischievously. She saw her aunt turn pink in turn and, giving the other woman's arm an affectionate squeeze, added, "I think Dr. Dudding's terrific. Are his intentions honorable?"

Her aunt made a face but dodged the teasing question by saying, "I've got to go into Farnham today. Care to come along for the ride?"

Susan nodded in agreement, and after the breakfast dishes had been taken care of, the two of them set off toward town, with Susan at the wheel. When they arrived, she dropped Ruth off at the dry cleaner's and then looked for a parking spot nearby. Her first task was to pick up the mail at the post office, so having parked the car she sprinted across the road to collect the bundle of letters and magazines. All but one letter was addressed to her aunt. The other letter bore Hilary's efficient, economical handwriting. Susan tore open the envelope eagerly. Hilary had written to say she was coming to visit for a week, bringing an update on all the gossip, and she asked if someone would please meet the five o'clock train on Friday. Susan was delighted at the prospect of her sister's visit. They hadn't seen each other for nearly two months, although they'd phoned and written each other regularly.

Her next stop was the hardware store. She greeted Mr. Sheldon and explained to him laughingly why she needed another gallon of green paint for the turkey coop. "Between Richard, me and the occasional renegade turkey, a fair amount of the paint never did get transferred successfully from the can to the coop," she concluded with a grin.

As Susan waited by the front counter for Mr. Sheldon to match the color of the paint, she heard someone behind her cough loudly. Turning around out of idle curiosity, Susan found herself looking into the cool, blue eyes of Lindy Barwick. But Lindy's gaze rested on her only for a second before she looked past Susan to the young lad behind the counter.

"Hi, Lindy, what can I help you with?" It was Andy Norman speaking.

Ignoring Susan completely, Lindy addressed herself to the young shop assistant. "Have those hooks I ordered last week arrived yet?"

The boy reached under the counter and brought out a small paper bag. Lindy counted out the required money, shoved the bag into her purse, and without so much as a nod to Susan, strode out of the hardware store.

Well, la-di-da, Susan thought wryly. *What did I do to deserve the cold shoulder, I wonder?*

Mr. Sheldon appeared with the paint a minute or two later, and after paying for it Susan made her way out the door. Mr. Sheldon's teasing voice called after her, "Don't trip now, young lady!"

She put the paint in the trunk of the Mini and turned around just as Ruth walked toward her, her arms full of dry cleaning and groceries. When those parcels, too, had been secured in the trunk, the two of them started to get into the car to head home for lunch.

"Oh, rats!" Ruth exclaimed. "I forgot to pick up some supplies I need to fix the fencing around the turkey coop. We'll have to go back to the hardware store again. Could you come along and help me carry a roll of wire?"

"Of course!" Susan answered, closing the door again and walking back to the curb.

The two women hadn't gone more than twenty yards up the street when a deafening explosion sent them instinctively onto their faces on the sidewalk. Pieces of glass sprayed around them, and a moment later they heard the crackle of flames.

"Aunt Ruth! Are you all right?" Susan's voice was taut with fear.

"I...I think so! What happened?"

They looked up cautiously, then stared in horror. The old Mini was unrecognizable. Flames were leaping from the shell that used to house the engine, and all the windows had blown out. What used to be shiny chrome had been reduced to a black hulk.

The explosion had damaged the car parked in front of the Mini as well, crumpling the fender and searing the light blue finish.

"C'mon, let's get out of here!" Susan helped Ruth to her feet and the two of them quickly moved further away from the blazing car. From what they felt was a safe distance they turned and, in shock, watched the clouds of black smoke rising from the remains of the little car.

Almost instinctively they grasped each other's arms, both women numb with the realization that by rights they should have been in the Mini when the explosion happened—that only by a fluke had their very lives been spared.

A crowd of onlookers had gathered within

seconds, and before long they heard the authoritative voice of a policeman ordering people to move back

"What happened?" someone shouted, and as Susan went forward to talk to the police officer, she heard an old lady say matter-of-factly, "It's a bomb. These crazy terrorists...."

Susan looked at the woman in horror, until the police officer noticing her terrified expression, said, "Don't pay the woman any mind, miss. "The old dear lost a couple of sons in the army, and I'm afraid it's affected her mind. She thinks the whole world is peopled with terrorists." The policeman's voice was sympathetic; he hadn't written off the woman as a lunatic, but he was obviously used to her frequent public statements on bombings.

"Have y-you...had any bombings here?" Susan asked hesitantly, still more than a little dismayed by the old woman's comments.

"Not one, miss, until now. Are you the owner of the car?" Seeing that his fellow officers had cordoned off the still-smoking vechicle and were holding the crowd of villagers back to a safe distance, the police officer took out his black notebook and began jotting down the details of the incident.

Susan explained what had happened, then looked around for her aunt so that she could add more particulars. But she couldn't see the older woman anywhere. "Aunt Ruth," she called, and heard the note of hysteria in her own voice. "Aunt Ruth!" *Don't cry, Susan Baker*, she told herself firmly. *Control yourself, this is not that serious. It has to be a mistake, a freak accident. It is not what you think it is—a deliberate attempt at murder.*

From out of the crowd her aunt appeared, Mr. Sheldon's arm around her comfortingly. "I'm here, love," she said quietly, her face still unnaturally pale. "I'll talk to the policeman now."

Wearily, Susan wandered through the crowd to find somewhere where she could sit down, or at least lean, and try to collect her scattered thoughts. "Oh, my God, not again...." She closed her eyes and leaned against the cool brick of one of the shops farther down from the hardware store.

A few minutes later she opened her eyes, focusing them on the equestrian shop across the street. As her eyes adjusted, she saw a familiar figure hurry across the street, now jammed with cars, and head toward her.

"Susan! My dear! What happened?"

"You know, Dr. Dudding, I have absolutely no idea." Susan cast around for words of explanation that would not sound too absurd. "We'd...been shopping, just running a few errands, and when we went to the hardware store for the last time...the Mini blew up...."

"Ruth..." the doctor said, his eyes registering his horror.

"She's fine. Aunt Ruth is fine; I left her talking to the policeman, but we should go to her...."

Dr. Dudding took Susan's arm gently and steered her through the dispersing crowd to where Aunt Ruth stood, watching a fireman douse the last of the flames with foam.

"Hello, Stephen," she greeted the doctor quietly, not seeming in the least surprised to see him. "My niece and I are in the market for a ride back to Grasshopper Hill. Would you mind terribly if—"

"Of course I'll drive you," Dr. Dudding interrupted brusquely. Susan recognized the tone he adopted unconsciously when he was genuinely worried about something, and she joined her aunt in thanking him gratefully as they all walked to his car.

"I was just driving through town when I saw smoke and the crowd of people. I thought a doctor might be needed so I stopped immediately. Thank God I did, "Stephen Dudding concluded, looking at Ruth worriedly. He put a hand over hers, which was clasped limply on her lap as she sat silently beside him in his old Austin. "We'll be at the farm in no time, Ruth," he added softly, and Susan caught a glimpse of tenderness in his eyes as he looked at her aunt.

Once back at Grasshopper Hill, the doctor gave them both a quick examination and confirmed that, apart from minor shock and a very bad scare, they were both fine. "Take it easy you two," he warned as he seated Ruth in one of the armchairs in the living room and gently covered her legs with a large yellow blanket. "You've both had a nasty scare. You're going to have to stay quiet for a while and not excite yourselves."

Not a word of argument came from either of the two women as they sat back, numbed and exhausted, in their chairs. Dr. Dudding looked worriedly at both of them. They were too subdued for his liking—unnaturally so, even considering the circumstances.

He moved toward the brandy decanter at the far end of the living room, then turned as he heard the front door flung open. Richard Evans strode in, his expression clearly alarmed.

"I saw Ruth's Mini—or what's left of it—being towed down the main street in Farnham just now," he said tersely. "What in blazes happened?"

The doctor smiled grimly at Richard's choice of words. "According to Susan, it blew up. Probably a bomb was planted, because cars don't just explode for no reason. Fortunately, neither she nor Ruth was hurt."

"God in heaven," Richard said through clenched teeth, walking quickly over to Susan. He took one of her hands between his own and spoke softly to her. "Are you all right, Susan? Oh, my dear...." he murmured, looking anxiously into her pale face.

Susan's eyes were large and fearful as she looked at Richard. Her voice no more than a hoarse whisper, she said, "I think someone...is trying to kill me."

Chapter 10

"Let's not jump to any conclusions," Richard admonished quietly, but Susan could see the worry in his eyes. "Try to relax," he went on, "there could be any number of reasons for that explosion. I'll talk to the police and the mechanic as soon as they've had a chance to look at it. Right now, just follow the good doctor's orders and try to stay quiet. Shall I help you to bed or will you be all right down here?"

"Of course I'll be all right," Susan murmured, her lips curving in a half smile. "I just have to convince myself—"

"Shh, no more talk like that. Would you like me to stay with you a while longer?"

Susan wished with all her heart that Richard would stay. She longed to just sit and listen to his deep, gentle voice allaying her fears. She knew he was busy, however, and that he no doubt had at least one appointment for that afternoon. "No, Richard," she said at last. "Thank you for coming by. It was very thoughtful of you, but I'm fine now, really." She turned her head away from him, unable to meet the worry in his green eyes.

He rose slowly from the seat he had drawn up beside her, and she felt herself grow dizzy as he put his hand behind her head and kissed her gently on the lips. "I'll look in on you this evening," he murmured, and in two long strides he was gone from the room.

Dr. Dudding saw Richard out, then returned to help Ruth up to her bedroom. "I suggest you take a cue from your aunt and go up to bed, too, Susan," the doctor said firmly. "Your system has had quite a shock." He had been relieved that neither Susan nor Ruth had seen the look of smoldering fury on Richard's face as he left. He knew that further worry would only aggravate their condition, and he was anxious for them to rest as completely as possible.

Susan gave a wan smile of acquiescence and followed her aunt and Dr. Dudding up the stairs. Ruth had been quiet all the while Richard had been with Susan, but there had been a look of deep concern on her face as she'd watched the exchange between Richard and her niece.

Closing the curtains in her bedroom to shut out the bright afternoon sun, Susan kept repeating to herself that the whole thing was only an accident. As she dropped off to sleep she heard the phone ringing in the kitchen below, and then Dr. Dudding's deep voice answer, "No, neither of them is in any condition to talk to reporters right now...."

When she awoke several hours later, her first thought was of her Aunt Ruth. Hastily climbing back into her sundress and running a comb through her hair, she walked the length of the upstairs hall to her aunt's bedroom. But there was no sign of the woman and the bed had been remade so perfectly that it didn't look at all as if it had recently been slept in. Giving a mental thumbs up sign to her stalwart aunt, Susan went downstairs to the kitchen, but that room, too, was empty. Curious now as to her whereabouts, Susan walked out the kitchen door to the backyard. The sun was still bright even though it was after six o'clock, and Susan held a hand to her face to shade her eyes. At the far end of the garden she caught sight of her aunt, who was training a hose on her rose bushes with one hand. With the other hand she was gesticulating animatedly to another person, with whom she appeared to be deep in conversation. Only when the other person, who was half-hidden by a rose bush, took a few steps backward did Susan recognize Richard. With a rush of pleasure she walked over to the two of them.

"Nothing, absolutely nothing, comes between you and your gardening, eh, Aunt Ruth?" Susan teased, putting her arm around the woman's waist.

"Amazing, isn't she?" Richard added in unconcealed admiration. "And what about you, Susan. . .?"

"Oh, I'm fine," she put in hastily. In reality she was almost sick with worry, but she knew if she told Richard about her suspicions he'd probably reprimand her for letting her imagination run away again. He gave her a piercing look, however, before turning back to her aunt with a comment about her rose garden and about the various hybrids she was growing so successfully. Susan was relieved he no longer seemed too concerned about the incident that had happened earlier in the afternoon. If Richard had no reason to be concerned, Susan thought with a shrug, then neither had she.

"How about a drink at the Blue Bell after dinner, Sue?" Richard asked, turning toward her again. "I have a bit of paperwork to do now; would it be okay if I pick you up around eight o'clock?"

"A lovely idea," she agreed, her eyes large and very blue as she smiled up at him. Susan watched him walk back across the lawn to his car. Pleasure and eager anticipation surged through her, as she wished she could move the hands of her wristwatch ahead two hours.

RICHARD ARRIVED a few minutes after eight and was conversing idly in the kitchen with Ruth when Susan came down the stairs. She had taken a lot of care in dressing for the evening, and she flushed with pleasure at the look on Richard's face as his gaze took in her navy blue and white cotton skirt and the white appliquéed blouse that complemented it. The blue of her skirt was almost the same color as her eyes, and the white cotton contrasted pleasingly with her golden throat and face. Her skin had acquired a rosy tan from the many hours she spent riding and gardening, and with the chestnut highlights in her rich brown hair, she looked radiantly lovely.

Richard didn't have to say a word; his look was enough to warm Susan to the core. His expression was openly sensuous and her cheeks grew redder as she saw as well as felt his scrutiny.

"Shall we go?" he said at last.

Susan had believed that all thought of the day's mishap had left his mind, but as she looked across at him as he drove toward the Blue Bell, she knew that he was worried about something.

"You're frowning," she said lightly, hoping that he might tell her what was on his mind. "It can't be something I said, because I haven't said a word!"

He didn't answer, but turned to smile at her, and put a hand over hers.

"I haven't been to the Blue Bell since I was eighteen," Susan said, trying to fill the silence and disguise the worry that his expression was beginning to cause her. "You took me there for a drink on my eighteenth birthday, remember?"

"Yes, Sue, I remember," he replied, giving her hand a squeeze.

What is he thinking about, she wondered, *I feel so cut off from him.... He's miles away. Is he thinking about this afternoon?*

They arrived at the Blue Bell, where Richard ordered a Dubonnet and lemonade for Susan and a pint of lager for himself.

"Richard," Susan began quietly after they had gotten their drinks, "please tell me what's wrong."

Richard put down the beer mug he was holding, lighted a cigarette and stared at Susan intently for a moment, watching her brow slowly wrinkle in concern as she looked back at him.

"I spoke to the mechanic this afternoon," he said curtly, as well as to the police. "What happened today was no accident. Someone planted a hand-made bomb under the fender of your aunt's Mini."

"No!" Susan's hand flew to her mouth, her eyes wide with horror. "No! Who...." She leaned back against the padded, red-leather chair and looked at Richard in disbelief. "Who is...trying to kill me...?"

"I've been wondering that very thing ever since this afternoon," Richard replied grimly. "But nothing seems to make any sense."

"There're so many horrible things happening, maybe none of them are accidents.... By the way, why didn't you confront Andy Norman after the incident in your oasthouse?" Susan asked, still shaken by the knowledge of what had to be a deliberate murder attempt that afternoon.

"The reason I didn't say anything was that I wanted to find out conclusively who put Andy up to it. He's just a kid, you know. He's been in and out of trouble ever since he was little, and he's only fifteen now. His mother does the best she can, but she's had to work ever since her husband left her. I guess she just hasn't been around enough to discipline the boy. She's a good lady, though, hardworking and honest—I'd be lost without her running my office.

"Anyhow, I've spoken to Morris Sheldon, the fellow who owns the hardware store in town, about him—who the boy sees and so on. You know Andy works there part-time?" Susan nodded. "Well, Morris couldn't help much. He said the kid kept pretty well to himself and, as far as he knew, didn't seem to meet any of the other boys after work."

Richard rubbed a hand over his eyes, then took another sip of his beer. He looked exhausted and Susan's heart went out to him.

"Have you spoken to his mother?" she asked gently.

"I don't want to involve Sarah at this stage, if I can help it. She has enough on her plate right now."

"Maybe Andy would talk to me," Susan suggested.

"No, Susan," Richard replied firmly. "I'd prefer it if you didn't approach him. I don't want him to be on his guard. He's a wily kid, full of what the Americans call 'street smarts.' He'd get the better of you, and you wouldn't even know it. You'd come back to me saying the boy is as innocent as a babe in arms."

"I'd like to think I haven't been that sheltered," Susan protested. "I'm not totally naive, you know."

"All I'm saying," Richard persisted gently, "is that some people are devious and crafty and you'd never know it to look at them. Morris Sheldon says Andy's one of the best assistants he's had in years."

"Getting back to this afternoon," Susan said, "how could they tell there had been a bomb? How did they know the engine didn't explode because of some mechanical failure? And wouldn't all the evidence be destroyed in the explosion?"

"To begin with, they found a starter cap under

the car. There usually are bits and pieces left around after a bomb goes off—the timing device and things like that. The most obvious proof, of course, was the damage to the car itself. There just isn't anything near the left side of the front fender of a Mini that could possibly blow a hole like that."

"Any idea of who might have done it? I mean, right in downtown Farnham in the middle of the day?"

"Anybody could have. It's the kind of bomb that a kid could make, and you can fix them so that they just clip on under the fender. It would be a matter of ten seconds' work. I'm sure many mechanics have seen the results of these things at some time or other."

Kids...a bomb that kids could make....Susan put down her glass slowly, a sudden thought dawning on her. "Richard," she said, nearly choking on her drink. "You don't think that Andy Norman...."

"I confess the same thought occurred to me," he replied shortly. "But I spoke to Morris Sheldon and he told me that Andy was in the store all day."

Susan's expression cleared, and with a sigh of relief she remembered having seen Andy in the shop right before the explosion. He'd been serving Lindy. She sipped her Dubonnet and accepted the cigarette Richard offered her.

"Susan...I know I have no right to ask this," he began awkwardly, "but you mentioned that you'd had a little grief before leaving London, and though you've never elaborated on it, I presume whatever happened to some extent prompted your decision to move to Grasshopper Hill for a while."

"That's true," Susan murmured, hoping he wasn't going to ask her to explain the situation between herself and Peter.

Richard took both her hands in his and said ear-

nestly, "I know it must be painful, or you wouldn't
be avoiding the subject, but in the light of what's
happening to you here, I'm going to ask you to tell
me what made you decide to come back. Something—any small thing—might help us to understand what's going on. Please, Susan, for your own
sake...."

Susan freed her hands so that she could push her
hair behind her shoulders in a self-conscious ges-
ture, then she bit her lip, wondering where to start.
Stop making an issue of it, she berated herself. *What's at
stake here except your foolish pride?*

"I—I don't know if you were aware that I'd applied to Oxford," she began hesitantly. She looked
at Richard, and when she saw he wasn't laughing at
her, she went on more easily, her reticence ebbing
with a newfound desire to share this part of her life
with him. She explained how she had failed the
Oxbridge exam, how immensely disappointed she
had been and how she had subsequently argued
with Peter.

He listened without interrupting until the end,
when she explained the incident in the restaurant
where she and Peter had nearly come to blows.
Then Richard threw back his head and laughed.
"I'm sorry!" he exclaimed. "But I can just see you!"

"What on earth are you talking about?" Susan
asked, a little put out that Richard found her argument with Peter so amusing.

"I'm not laughing at you, I'm just remembering
your temper. Do you recall the time Hilary bor-
rowed your tennis racket and you thought I had
hidden it from you?"

"And I stormed at you for five minutes!" Susan
breathed, then giggled as she remembered how
foolish she'd felt when Hilary had returned it.

Richard laughed again and Susan joined him.

"My, but you were in a rage. You didn't forget

your manners, though," he teased. "You were very careful to say you were sorry."

"I'm just glad I'm not thirteen again," Susan said contritely. "Or seventeen, either."

"You've changed a lot in the interim, I must say. But I was fond of that skinny little girl you used to be."

Susan flushed.

"Why did you stop coming to Grasshopper Hill, Susan?" Richard asked softly.

She averted her eyes, unable to meet his probing gaze. "I...thought I'd outgrown it," she stated humbly. "I'd just met Peter and I thought I was too sophisticated for the country." She looked at Richard, shamefaced, then went on determinedly. "I've grown up since then, I think. I seem to have grown through a lot of the ideas I had for a while."

"And Peter?" Richard asked quietly.

"I...I'm not sure. He's written to me once or twice asking me to come back to London...."

"And?"

"I told him I needed more time. I'm not quite sure what my plans are for the future."

"You love the country, don't you, Susan?"

"Yes," she murmured. "I've been very happy for the last couple of months—very much at peace...."

Richard looked at her for a long moment, but his expression was unreadable. Finally he looked at his watch and said, "We'd better go; it's nearly closing time."

THOUGH SHE had felt relaxed enough when Richard saw her to the door at the end of the evening, Susan's overwrought nerves gave her nightmares all night, and, hollow eyed and pale, she crept down to the kitchen well before six the next morning to make some coffee. Her aunt, already on her second cup, looked at Susan with concern, noting her almost hunted look.

"Richard told me what the police said," her aunt stated quietly, without preamble. "That's what we were talking about in the garden yesterday when you joined us. I don't know what to say, darling. Do you think you ought to return to London?"

Susan looked at her aunt wearily as she poured the coffee into her cup. "No," she said firmly. "I'm not going to give in. I will not have some demented person—or a series of accidents—drive me away. I love it here, Aunt Ruth, and I want to be able to come back any time I want."

"Perhaps you could go just for a little while," Ruth suggested. "Wait till this blows over, then come back...."

"How can it blow over?" Susan retorted, her nerves raw. "We don't even know what's going on, or if someone really is out to get me. Whoever this 'crazy' is, that is, if it all isn't just a string of terrible coincidences, he seems to be after me, or people connected with me. Look at the pattern: I'm in a half-constructed house, and I fall and nearly break my neck. I ride a horse and it dies. I'm driving a car and it gets a bomb planted in it. Oh, my gosh—what else?" she concluded bitterly, covering her face with her hands.

Ruth got up from her chair. That was all that was needed for Susan to let go of her last ounce of reserve, and leaning against her aunt she began to sob. She cried as if she wouldn't ever stop, and then, almost choking, she whispered, "Aunt Ruth, I'm so scared...."

Finally she had cried herself out, and with a weak smile she left the kitchen and headed back to her bedroom, hoping that this time she would be exhausted enough to sleep.

But again oblivion was denied her. Images whirled wildly through her brain—the burned Mini, the glazed eyes of Champion, the splintered floorboards of the oasthouse—until Susan finally curled up in a ball on her bed, covered her face with her hands and pressed until her fingers were white. "Stop!" she cried. "For God's sake, stop!"

By early evening Susan had developed a fever, and by the time Dr. Dudding arrived she had already been moved to the room Ruth had made up for Hilary.

"I wanted to get her into fresh sheets, Stephen," Susan dimly heard her aunt explaining. "Poor thing has been thrashing around so much, they're not only wet, they're also all askew."

Susan was not aware of what the doctor replied, but she was grateful for the cool cloth he put on her forehead a minute or two later.

"There's no reason," she murmured to him—perfectly matter-of-factly, she thought," for someone to want to kill me. Absolutely no reason...." Then the injection he gave her began to take effect and she closed her eyes. "The bomb...there was no reason, you see...."

The fever lasted only twenty-four hours, a result, the doctor explained to her later, of overwrought nerves and total mental exhaustion.

"Richard was up to see you twice, but you didn't seem to recognize him," her aunt said, sitting at the end of Susan's bed the next evening, a cup of tea in her hand.

"I don't remember him being here, I must admit," Susan said, eating the omelet her aunt had prepared for her.

"He said you kept repeating the words 'gas station.' Do you remember what it was in particular you were thinking about?"

Susan reflected for a moment, trying to piece together the fragments of the horrible, recurring dream she had had. "I kept driving somewhere," she began, looking out her bedroom window as she tried to conjure up the dream. "And every time I went to...this place, this person would grin at me...." She shuddered at the memory. "It was a horrible, evil grin, and the person would repeat the words 'that will teach you.' That's all he ever said. It was awful! But I can't picture the face. You know how in dreams people can be faceless...? You think you recognize them, but when you try to recall what they looked like, it's just a blank...." Susan shivered again, then looked at her aunt. "I'm going to try to remember more of that dream. I feel that there's more to it than I understand at this stage. It's as if my subconscious is offering me something that my conscious isn't willing to accept. Does that make any sense?"

"Yes, Sue, it does," her aunt said quietly. "Many admissions—realizations, home truths—make themselves known to us in that way. It's always been my belief that our perceptions run much deeper than the first level of consciousness. It's as if we know things that we aren't even aware we know. Our conscious mind, which has our best interests at heart, accepts into its awareness only those things it figures we are capable of dealing with. But sometimes the screening process goes a bit awry, and perceptions jump into our first level of consciousness that we're not yet ready to accept or deal with. I suspect that's when breakdowns occur—that can run the whole gamut from nightmares to insanity."

The two women remained quiet for a few minutes, both lost in thought. Then Ruth removed the tray from Susan's bed, kissed her niece good-night and left the room, turning off the overhead light as she went.

Chapter 11

Susan arrived at the station in Farnham just as the train was pulling in. She'd been gardening with her aunt all afternoon and the time had flown by, unnoticed by either of them. Showering quickly and throwing a yellow flowered sundress over her head, Susan had rushed out to the car Ruth had rented in lieu of her Mini, and she had driven to the station as quickly as she dared. It seemed in retrospect that she and the train had coordinated their timing perfectly.

After only a few minutes, Susan caught sight of her sister stepping down from the train.

"Hill, darling, you're looking great! How lovely to see you again!" she cried, heading toward her.

Hilary hugged her sister affectionately and raised an eyebrow at the shiny new car that Susan led her to. "Moving up in the world, are we?" she suggested with a grin.

"There's a long and rather bizarre story attached to this car, Hilly," Susan said lightly, "and it's not one I feel like going into now. I'll save it till I've got the strength," she added quickly, noting the odd look her sister gave her.

The two of them chattered all the way back to

Grasshopper Hill, catching up on each other's news and exchanging memories of past summer holidays spent at the Coleman farm. Susan was a little more subdued than usual, but if her sister was aware of it, she refrained from commenting.

"How do you always manage to look so elegant and cool, Hilly?" Susan demanded. "After a frantic day in London and a steamy train ride out of harassed, hysterical Waterloo Station, you appear in Farnham as beautiful and relaxed as if you'd stepped off the cover of a magazine. What's your secret?"

"First off," Hilary said, keeping a remarkably straight face, "it's all done with mirrors." When Susan giggled, she insisted, "Honestly, Susie, it's all an illusion."

"Oh, all right, keep your damn trade secrets!"

"One word of advice, my dear, just one word: Permapress."

Susan's giggle turned to a peal of laughter and she turned to grin at her sister. "I'm delighted you've come for a visit, Hilly. I've missed you!"

For a day or two, Susan was able to push all thoughts of the murder attempts out of her mind—during daylight at least. Even though she and Hilary were having a wonderful time, talking non-stop and frequently breaking into gales of laughter, when nighttime came Susan found herself being swallowed up again in an abyss of fear and suspicion. Since the incident with the car earlier in the week, nothing untoward or unusual had happened. But then Susan hadn't once left Grasshopper Hill, apart from picking up her sister at the train station.

She reflected a great deal on what her aunt had said about the subconscious knowing things that the conscious dared not acknowledge, and she struggled repeatedly to recall the dream about the person with the chilling smile. Susan was convinced more than ever that that dream was a key to the mysterious, terrifying occurrences that had been happening.

On Sunday night Susan had the nightmare again. But on this occasion, one or two details of the dream changed. She was in the Mini, but for some absurd reason, she was driving it into the stables at Lindesfarne. She applied the brake to stop, but suddenly Champ darted in front of the car, and with a deep thud, the car struck the animal. "You've killed her!" a voice screamed. "You've killed Champion!" Horrified and trembling, Susan got out of the car and went over to the inert body of the mare. "You'll pay for this," the same voice shrieked venomously, and when Susan turned around she saw that her car was in flames. "That'll teach you...."

She awoke with a start, to find her heart was racing and her body was covered in sweat. Her hair was damp around her forehead as well, and she knew from the salty taste in her mouth that she'd been crying.

"What is happening to me?" she whispered wretchedly. "These dreams will drive me mad.... If I could only understand their meaning and accept the information in them, I know I'd be free of it. I know it!"

When Susan finally drifted off again, her sleep was deep and dreamless.

"GOOD MORNING, Susie! Lady Wilhemina and I have come to visit!"

Susan opened an eye reluctantly and saw her sister's slim body clad in jodhpurs and a soft pink close-fitting shirt. She then opened the other eye to watch the wolfhound leap joyously onto her bed. The mattress springs and Susan groaned at the same time.

"What's the time, Hilly?" she asked drowsily.

"Seven-fifteen," Hilary replied promptly. "It's a beautiful day and I'm in the mood for a long gallop across the fields."

"Right now?" Susan asked skeptically.

"Can you think of a better time?"

"Yes, any time later in the day! Go and be pleasant to Aunt Ruth for a while. Willie and I have some snoozing to do."

Hilary shrugged good-naturedly, and called over her shoulder as she was leaving the room, "If you're not down in an hour I'm leaving without you!"

By eight o'clock Susan had managed to make herself presentable and was down in the kitchen with Hilary and Ruth nursing a cup of freshly brewed coffee. She noticed the look on her aunt's face as she said good-morning, and with a small smile acknowledged that what her aunt suspected was true: she'd had another nightmare. By common consent neither she nor Ruth had said anything to Hilary, thinking it best for her own sake that she be kept out of the situation and spared the worry.

As things turned out, however, Hilary was very soon made aware of the mysterious "events," as Ruth termed them. The two sisters drove to Lindesfarne for their morning ride, and by prior arrangement had planned to go on from there to visit Richard Evans and his sister, Gilly, who had just returned home for summer vacation.

As they drove up the laneway to the farm, they saw Rafe near the stables and they waved at him.

"Well, now, the second Miss Baker," the old man said with a twinkle. "How are you, Hilary?"

"As well as can be, thank you, Rafe. It's great to be back—though I'm only here for a week, I regret to say "

"The call of the bright lights, I suppose," Rafe commented dryly.

"Any horses in need of some exercise, Rafe?" Susan asked.

"Well, now, Susan, let me think. Now that I no longer have Champion or Big Tiger—"

"What?" Susan put in quickly. "What about Big Tiger? I...I thought he'd gotten better. I'd heard—"

"Sure enough seemed to," Rafe replied, shaking his head, "then suddenly he took a turn for the worse. We lost him, too."

"But Champion died over two weeks ago," Susan went on, ignoring her sister's astonished reaction to the exchange. "When did Big Tiger.... Why didn't I hear about it?"

"You haven't been here for about two weeks, Susie," Rafe reminded her gently. "What with your accidents—"

"Susan!" Hilary's firm voice interrupted. "Just exactly what has been going on here? Two dead horses, accidents...."

"I'm sorry, Susie," Rafe muttered apologetically. "I didn't realize...."

"Don't worry, Rafe," she said quickly, "We were hoping that Hilary—"

"For heaven's sake, Susan—" concern made Hilary's voice harsh "—fill me in on what's been happening."

"I'll tell you when we've saddled up," Susan conceded. "Is there anything for us to ride, Rafe?"

"All the other horses are out, I'm afraid. Lindy Barwick's out on Moonlight and young Sally Morton is riding Kinsman. Why not try the stables down the road? They'll probably have some horses available, since they have a bigger outfit than I do."

They thanked Rafe and got back in the car; a few minutes later they reached the stables Rafe had referred to. Susan knew the owner vaguely, and leaving Hilary in the car, she went into the stable. A few minutes later she emerged, a bleak look on her face.

"What did he say?" her sister asked, troubled by the expression on Susan's face.

"He said," she replied in a small voice, "that he'd heard about the deaths of Rafe's horses and that he was terribly sorry but he didn't feel comfortable about letting me ride one of *his* own horses."

"What rot!" Hilary burst out, anger darkening her eyes. "That's tantamount to blaming you for the death of those two horses! Why, that's slander!"

Susan threw her sister a look of such utter desolation that Hilary leaned over and put an arm around her. "I don't know the details, Susie," she said fiercely, "but it's vicious of him to have said what he did to you. I'm going to stay here at Farnham until I get to the bottom of all this!"

Susan gave Hilary a hug, and with a teary smile suggested they go over to the Evans's. "I'd like to see Gilly again." she said. "She'll cheer us up."

They had agreed to meet Richard at one, and since they arrived considerably earlier than that, only Gillian was there to greet them.

"Enter the lovely Baker sisters!" she said with the wide, friendly smile that they always associated with her.

Gilly was still unabashedly a tomboy. Though her body was showing the shape and promise of a blossoming femininity, she fought it vigorously, refusing to wear anything except faded blue jeans and bulky sweaters.

Susan realized she hadn't seen Richard's sister since Gilly had become a teenager, and she was visibly startled by the change in her. Naturally enough she had grown considerably, and as her face filled out she looked more than ever like her brother. Her hair, still hanging in one long braid behind her back, was much lighter than her brother's, however, and where his eyes were sea green, hers were a clear, warm gray. Her freckles had for the most part disappeared, and so had the braces on her teeth.

"Pleased to be back, Gilly?" Hilary asked, giving an affectionate tug to her braid.

"School," Gilly announced vehemently, "along with cooked carrots and Lindy Barwick, ought to be outlawed."

"My, my," Hilary remarked mildly. "Such harsh words! The first two I would endorse wholeheartedly, but why the hostility toward our dear Lindy?"

"Because," Gilly stated, throwing herself onto the living-room sofa, "our dear Lindy is still trying to ingratiate herself with my brother. Not only that, she's even trying to curry favor with old Mrs. Norman!"

Susan felt her insides give a slight lurch, and keeping her eyes fixed on one of the grass stains on her jodhpurs, she asked Gilly casually, "What makes you think she's doing that?"

"For heaven's sake, Susan," Gilly said, making a display of rolling her eyes. "I only got home on Saturday, and she's already been here twice—once to see Richard and once on the sly to see Mrs. Norman. That second visit is meant to be a secret, though," she giggled. "I saw her going in the side entrance, where Richard's office is. Honestly, who does she think she's fooling?"

"Probably Richard," Hilly pointed out blandly.

"Oh, I have an idea he knows," Gilly replied with a shrug. "Lindy is about as subtle as a car accident. Remember the time...."

Susan listened only half-attentively to Gilly's story about Lindy and a broken bridle. The other half of her attention was focused on the girl's casual comment that Lindy had been over to visit Richard. Had he invited her? Susan didn't know if their friendship was that close. That Lindy was still living with her aunt, Lucy Whilsmith, Susan was aware. She also knew that, according to Mrs. Whilsmith, Lindy didn't seem to be making the slightest effort to find her own accommodation. Was she deliberately staying out in Bordon to be near Richard? Susan found herself fervently hoping that that wasn't the case. She preferred to think that Lindy was simply trying to save a little money so she could properly furnish a flat when she found one. *And visiting Mrs. Norman, as well*, Susan mused. *Heavens, what a blantant approach! Or, perhaps what a clever one....*

Susan forced her attention back to Gilly and Hilary, and joined in their conversation about the upcoming horse show.

Another hour flew by, and before they knew it they heard Richard's step in the front hall. "A room full of lovely ladies, how delightful," he commented with a grin.

"Hello, Richard. My, I'd forgotten how attractive you are. No wonder Susan came back to you!" Hilary said, disarmingly forthright as usual.

Susan felt herself grow hot under Richard's amused and faintly surprised look, and she heard Gilly give a loud groan.

"Not a very ladylike sound, young Gillian," Richard said in mock reproof. "If words escape you I suggest you remain quiet!"

"I suggest I get us all a glass of wine," she retorted impudently.

"And I suggest you get wine for us and lemonade for yourself!"

Susan and Hilary exchanged amused glances at the cross fire, both of them sensitive to the exceptional closeness that existed between Richard and Gillian, a closeness that had no doubt been precipitated by the death of their parents.

"Been out riding, you two?" Richard asked casually, accepting the glass of wine Gilly offered him.

"Actually, no," Susan said hesitantly. "Richard... did you know that Big Tiger was dead?"

"No!" he said, visibly startled.

"Rafe told us this morning. I had heard he was getting better, but Rafe said he got worse again and died...the same way as Champion did."

"Susan—" Gilly began, her gray eyes wide.

"What else did he say," Richard cut in firmly.

"He suggested we try to get horses at the stables up the road...."

"Roger Bacon's place," Richard supplied, nodding.

"Well, we went there as Rafe suggested, but—"

"But the old so-and-so wouldn't let Susan take out one of his horses," Hilary finished with asperity, her previous anger resurging. "He said he'd heard about Rafe's horses dying, and he as much as accused Susan of killing them!"

"I see," Richard said quietly. Susan recognized the tension in his voice, however, and threw her sister a look that warned her to hold her peace.

"Will someone tell me what's going on?" Gilly asked finally. "My curiosity is killing me."

Briefly Richard explained about the mysterious deaths of Champion and Big Tiger, turning to Hilary as well when it became obvious that she hadn't heard the story, either.

"Did Dr. Fairweather ever figure out the cause?" Gilly asked.

Richard shook his head. "I called him a week ago, but the blood and tissue samples were still at the lab being analyzed."

"Well, call him again!" Gilly said vehemently. "It's unthinkable that Susan should be accused of killing horses. In fact, I'll call him myself right now," she added, jumping up from the sofa.

She returned a minute or two later to say that, according to the receptionist, the vet was out, but he would return her call when he got in.

Susan gave Gilly an affectionate smile. Horses were Gilly's life, and she knew she had a stalwart ally in the young girl.

"Rafe said something about you having accidents as well," Hilary said as the four of them went into the dining room for lunch. "Apart from the horses, what else has been happening?"

Reluctantly Susan recounted the story of her fall at the oasthouse that Richard was converting, and then about the bomb that had been planted in Ruth's Mini the week before. The horror of the two accidents returned vividly to Susan's mind, and she shivered at the memories.

"Come back to London with me at the end of the week, Susan," Hilary said firmly. "It certainly seems like there's someone around here who's out to get you...."

"Have you called the police, Susan?" Gilly wanted to know.

"There's no evidence, other than circumstantial," Richard told his sister grimly. "The police investigated the explosion in the Mini, of course, but they have no idea who planted it and very few clues to go on. Apparently it was an amateur job—something anyone could rig up—but unfortunately effective all the same. It could have been kids, or terrorists—anyone—but that's harder to prove than almost anything they deal with."

"What about the incident in the oasthouse?" Gilly persisted. "They might have been able to find out something."

"There were no witnesses, Gillian," Richard replied bitterly. "No one saw anything. The house is actually quite secluded. I asked around myself and, of course, questioned my foreman and the carpenters. But we're no further ahead than when it happened."

"Susan, please come back to London with me," Hilary said urgently. "I don't think it's safe for you here. There must be a maniac around somewhere...."

"No, Hilly," Susan said quietly. "I don't want to get so alarmed that I run away before I'm sure there's something to run from."

"I think what Susan wants to do," Richard told Hilary, looking at her older sister for confirmation, "is to get to the root of these strange occurrences once and for all. She loves it here...don't you Susan?"

"I certainly do."

There didn't seem to be anything further to say, and subdued, the four of them returned to the living room with their coffee as the housekeeper began to clear away the dishes. They had just seated themselves when the telephone rang. Gilly jumped up, but Richard put up a restraining hand. "I'll go," he said.

The three women waited in silence, hoping it was Dr. Fairweather on the phone so they could get a verdict regarding the horses. The tension they felt showed clearly on their faces.

After what seemed an interminable length of time, Richard walked slowly back into the living room. "That was the vet. The tests are back from the lab," he said, his voice expressionless.

"Well?" Gilly prodded impatiently.

"The horses were poisoned."

"With what?" Susan asked, her voice barely more than a whisper.

"Arsenic."

Chapter 12

Susan felt physically sick. She closed her eyes and dropped her head down so that her chin was resting almost against the base of her neck. Through her dizziness she heard the rest of them talking about the poisonings—about how Fowler's Solution, normally given to horses in minute doses as an appetite stimulant, could actually cause a lingering death if the dosage was increased dramatically, and how the lab had determined that that had been the cause of death of Rage's two horses. Dr. Fairweather had verified that the symptoms fitted those of a death by arsenic, mixed in increasing doses in the horses' feed over a period of time.

Though Susan was seated in one of the large armchairs beside the fireplace, she could feel her body start to sway. Then she felt a hand on her arm.

"It's all right, Susan," her sister murmured, "you know it's not your fault."

"But it was me who fed those horses before they died," she cried. "Me!" She lifted anguished eyes toward Richard, but he just gazed at her without speaking. *Oh, God,* she thought, *not you, too, Richard.* Did he, too, along with Roger Bacon and who knows else, suspect her? Susan felt it was more than she could bear.

"I think I'd better take her home," Hilary murmured. "She's overwrought."

Richard looked at Susan for a long moment, then said softly, "Are you all right? Would you like to go home?" His voice was subdued, and Susan felt as if she were being torn to shreds emotionally. She wondered wretchedly what the vet had said to him on the phone to cause this new aloofness on his part. She felt terribly alone; Richard had always seemed like such an ally to her....

Nodding dejectedly, she let Hilary lead her out the door to the rented car. Numbly she got inside and sat huddled in the front seat beside her sister.

When they arrived a few minutes later at Grasshopper Hill, Susan declined Hilary's offer of another cup of coffee. One look from Hilary must have quelled any incipient comment from Ruth as the two sisters made their way through the back door and upstairs to Susan's bedroom, because she watched the two figures in silence.

"Susie," Hilary said soothingly as she covered her with the eiderdown on the bed, "I'm going to give you one of the sleeping pills I take for my migraines. After you've slept for a bit, we can talk if you like. Right now, do your best to get your mind off of all these weird things that are going on, and try to sleep."

"'Sleep no more!'" Susan quoted wretchedly to herself, "'Macbeth does murder sleep! The innocent sleep, Sleep that knits up the ravel'd sleave of care.' Don't I wish...."

The pill her sister had given her was potent, however, and, mercifully for Susan, she slept soundly until dinnertime.

SUSAN GAZED absently out the window of the train, still wondering if she had been wise to succumb to the combined wishes of Hilary and her Aunt Ruth by returning to London.

The two of them had gone up to her bedroom that evening, having discovered she was awake, and had marshaled all their forces of persuasion to induce her to change her mind. Wearily she had agreed. She had lost her resilience, she knew, and was rapidly approaching a state of nervous exhaustion.

"What will I say to mom and dad?" Susan asked her sister dismally. "They don't know about any of this, you know. I never told them about my fall, or about the bomb. . . ."

"I know," Hilary replied. She thought for a minute, then brightened up. "Why not say you've come to visit Peter?"

Susan started. Peter. . . her reactions and feelings toward him were still very mixed. "I'm. . . not sure I want to see Peter."

"Don't then," came Hilary's matter-of-fact response. "Just tell the parents that you have. Go out and meet some of your girl friends or something, and tell mom and dad that you're out with Peter."

Susan gave her sister a weak smile. "You underestimate mother, Hilly. She'd see through me in a second."

"She might also be too tactful to comment," Hilary returned dryly.

Susan laid her head back against the seat and turned her sister's suggestion over in her mind. She tried to define exactly what her feelings now were toward Peter. Certainly she had loved him once—or thought she had. She remembered her first few weeks at Grasshopper Hill, how she had missed him a lot, and had on more than one occasion considered picking up the telephone to apologize for her outburst at the restaurant. But then, by the time his first letter arrived, the pain of missing him had lessened considerably and she had written back to say that she didn't want him to visit, at least not for a while.... That letter had prompted him to phone her up. He had talked for quite a while, pleading his case and swearing that he'd changed.

"Has he changed, Hilly?" Susan asked her sister curiously.

"Hard to say." Hilary shrugged and turned to stare out the window. "He's been over to the house a few times, but I haven't really seen that much of him, what with my exams at the school and all."

Despite her averted face, Susan could see from the reflection in the train window that Hilary was biting her lip, a self-conscious habit that always meant that she wasn't telling the whole truth. "Okay, Hilly, let it out! You're biting your lip, so you must be hiding something— something about Peter. Do you want to talk about it?"

Hilary laughed. "Caught again! One of these years I'm going to stop doing that. Actually, I'm a bit embarrassed about the whole thing."

"You're not hurting me, Hilly, if that's what you're afraid of," Susan said. "I'm not exactly pining away thinking about him, you know."

Hilary looked relieved, the self-conscious color leaving her face. "I didn't want to tell you," she laughed ruefully.

"Tell me what? Have you been out with him?"

"Yes, once or twice. When you left at the end of April he was beside himself, but whether it was his emotions or his ego in question, I won't speculate."

Susan caught the twinkle in Hilary's eyes and smiled. "I have an idea we both know the answer to that one!"

"In any case," Hilary went on, "he was furious—

but hurt, too, I think. He came over one night and talked about you for hours, trying to solicit my support on his behalf. He wanted me to justify some of his opinions, to tell him that he was not, in fact, old-fashioned, but that you were militant."

"Me? Militant?"

"Exactly!" Hilary said. "I told him I shared your views on most subjects, particularly vis-à-vis the right of women to pursue a career if they so chose.... Well, somehow that managed to sit well with him, even though I was effectively reiterating your position. My guess is that he saw secretarial college as less of a threat than Oxford, and thought I'd be less stubborn than you if he ever felt like getting serious with me. So he asked me out."

"And did he get serious?"

"I don't know; I never gave him the chance."

"Oh?" Susan was intrigued. She could easily picture Hilary in her no-nonsense way giving Peter a piece of her mind. "Come on, Hilly," she urged. "Tell!"

"You're not going to be pleased," she giggled guiltily. "I finally told him accountants give me hives!"

"Hilly!"

"Well, you asked...! Anyway, Sue, that was about a month ago, and, needless to say, that was the last I've seen of him."

The screech of metal wheels signaled the train's arrival in Waterloo Station and interrupted their laughter. As they dragged their bags down from the overhead rack, Susan asked Hilary if she had notified their parents that the two of them were coming.

"Oh, no," Hilary replied, casual as always, and Susan decided it was just as well as she didn't want to cause them any worry.

The rain clouds they'd left in Farnham had begun

to empty themselves over London, and turning up
the collars of their raincoats, the two sisters went
outside to join the line of people waiting for taxis.
"Remind me only to apply for jobs in the South
Seas," Hilary said, making a face. "I simply can't
imagine why people put up with this filthy
weather."

"Humbug, Hilly. It's been beautiful all summer.
Anyway, the farmers desperately need the rain,
according to Aunt Ruth."

"Well, let the rain fall on the farms, then, *not* on
my silky curls." Hilary's right hand went up to
assess the damage to her newly acquired hairdo.
She had had her hair cut just before going to the
country and still delighted in touching the bouncy
curls. Her hair had been long like Susan's, but it had
a natural wave in it, and when she had emerged
from the train at Farnham she'd been sporting a
short, caplike style, making her look considerably
more sophisticated than her nineteen years.

At last it was their turn for a taxi, and with relief
they bundled themselves into it and in unison gave
the driver their home address in Islington, just
north of London proper. Traffic, as usual, was congested, even though it was midafternoon, and the
combination of the crowded streets and pouring
rain stretched a twenty-minute ride into nearly
double that time.

Susan was looking forward to seeing her parents
again after an absence of almost two months, and
she felt her excitement quicken as the familiar
streets of the neighborhood came into view.

Islington was an interesting, mixed borough. It
boasted of wonderful, open-air Chapel Market,
which teemed with life every Saturday, as well as a
small fringe theater and some excellent local bistros. The architecture was primarily Georgian, and
extensive renovations of old houses were being

carried out to the extent that the local-government budget would allow. Cannonbury Square was particularly elegant for all the houses were beautifully kept up by their proud owners. It was in front of one of these houses that the taxi drew up.

A mixture of delight and amazement was expressed on Sheila Baker's face as she answered the furious ring of the doorbell a minute or two later. "What a surprise!" she said, opening wide the front door. "Both of you at once! Tea for two drowned rats?"

"I'll be down in five, mom," Hilary said, giving her mother a quick kiss before running upstairs to repair the damage to her shortened locks.

"I'd love some," Susan concurred. She gave her mother a hug, and pretended not to notice the older woman's second look at the dark circles under her eyes.

"Are you all right, Sue?"

"Fine, really," she replied quickly, making a mental note to do a skillful makeup job as soon as she had the opportunity.

Hilary came down to the living room just as Mrs. Baker put the tea tray down on the coffee table, repeating her favorite saying: "Not only is it raining, it's also wet out there!" Susan looked affectionately at her sister and saw that all traces of the damage that the weather had done to her hair had been repaired by a quick blast of her hair dryer. The odd thing about Hilly, Susan mused, was that even though she was scrupulously attentive to her appearance, no one could ever accuse her of being vain.

"Cup of tea, Hilly?" Mrs. Baker asked.

"Yes, please. And at least four pieces of that carrot cake I've been eyeing."

The three of them chattered animatedly as they had their tea, the two sisters passing on all the local

news from Grasshopper Hill. They had previously
agreed not to mention any of the incidents that had
been the reason for Susan's return to London. It
was difficult to tell, however, how perceptive their
mother actually was, and Susan intercepted more
than one odd look from her. When Mrs. Baker
casually inquired what had brought Susan home so
early in the summer, her heart gave a lurch.

"I missed you and dad," she said, unconscious of
the wistfulness in her smile. Though that was not
the real reason for her return, there was much
truth to her statement. She had missed her
parents.

She hoped her mother attributed her strained
appearance to the migraine she pleaded a short
while later—an excuse she used to retreat to the
solitude of her bedroom. The rainstorm had
arrived hand in hand with a drop in temperature,
and Susan snuggled gratefully under the covers of
her bed. As she lay there, she thought back to the
conversation she'd had with Hilary on the train,
and she smiled at the recollection of what Hilary
had said to Peter. Reflecting on the conversation,
Susan remembered that she had said, "You're not
hurting me, Hilly, if that's what you're afraid
of...." In fact it was true, but what interested her
most was how easily and spontaneously those
words had been spoken. It was mid-June now; had
she really been thinking of marrying Peter as
recently as two months ago? Or had she, subcon-
sciously, already made up her mind before that....
No, the thought of Peter and of the abrasive quarrel they had had no longer hurt her. But maybe she
should see him anyway, to find out if anything
remained of the feelings they had once had for one
another. His last letter had arrived during that
peaceful interval between Champion's death and
the car incident. In it he had written that he still

cared for her, but that he was following her cue and would wait until she got in touch with him before writing to her again. He had signed the letter "fondest love." *That doesn't mean a thing*, Susan thought.

She firmly resolved to think no more about Peter for the time being; there would be time enough for that later. It was far more important that she try to relax, and to that end she picked up the book on Chinese art that was lying on her bedside table and idly began to leaf through it.

THERE WERE four tiny men dressed in quilted jackets standing in a row, their feet encased in embroidered slippers. Each man was wearing beautifully crafted silk trousers as well. They were all talking at once, nearly toppling over each other in their eagerness to convince her of the validity of their arguments.

The two in scarlet trousers were advocating life in the city. They were shouting proverbs supporting their claim that only in the city were a citizen's wits sharpened; country life was for dull-witted peasants. The other two, who were clad in dazzling lemon yellow, argued that in the country a citizen would not need tricky words and a sharp tongue. The cities, they claimed, were full of devious people, whose values had been distorted by generations of living stacked up on top of each other like crickets in cages.

Becoming increasingly confused by their shouting, Susan wanted desperately to quiet their raucous voices. But just as she was about to speak they faded away, seeming to melt into a vast, richly decorated fire screen in the corner. Susan watched the screen in amazement, searching in vain for a flash of scarlet silk.

Then from the elaborate details of the fire screen

itself, a pattern began to emerge. It was the outline of a face. Slowly, steadily, it changed from an outline to a composite of various elements. The left side of the face was composed of bits and pieces of the London skyline, and Susan recognized the gate outside the university as well as part of the wicket in front of the Russell Square subway station. She caught a momentary flash of the neon sign that illuminated one corner of Trafalgar Square and a glimpse of the northern facade of Westminster Abbey.

Then the left side of the face began slowly to decompose, leaving only the merest outline, and the right side of the face emerged. This side was made up of little bits of the Hampshire countryside. An old stone wall formed the eybrow; the forehead was a gently rolling hill. The eye itself reflected a church spire, and on the cheek Susan could see Lindesfarne and Grasshopper Hill.

As she watched, the cheek and eye dissolved and only an outline was left. Susan looked at the outline of the whole face—and gasped. It was the face of Richard Evans. She tried to reach out and touch him, but the picture began to fade, turning yellow and then blue as it dissolved. And Susan's hands wouldn't move. They seemed to be weighed down by some massive object. She tried again to move them and the object seemed to shift and then slide. . . .

WITH A LOUD THUD, the art book slid from Susan's hands and landed on the floor. She started violently at the noise, then opened her eyes and looked around curiously. She was in her room in London and it was dark outside—that ominous, unnatural darkness of rainstorms. A glance at her bedside clock, however, told her it was just after five.

Rubbing her eyes, Susan climbed out of her cozy

bed to shut the window. She felt disoriented.
Though she knew perfectly well where she was,
she still felt as if part of herself was in another
world. It was the dream, of course. In confusion,
she tried to piece it together as she slowly got
dressed. A minute later, however, she heard her
father's voice, and with a rush of gladness she
hurried downstairs to greet him, all thoughts of
the dream banished from her mind.

Chapter 13

On the surface anyway, Susan's parents appeared to accept her explanation of why she had returned to London. She hadn't yet decided how long she intended to stay, and she was grateful that her parents didn't question her about it.

"It's lovely to have you back, darling, though I suspect you'll disappear again before we know it," her mother said at dinner that evening.

"Guess the country air was too rich for you, eh, Hilly?" Mr. Baker asked Hilary in the same dry tone that Aunt Ruth, his sister, so often adopted.

"Oh, you know me, dad," Hilary replied, with a mischievous grin. "I'm a confirmed city dweller. I thrive on noisy crowds and polluted air! Turkeys are fine but...."

"Pass your father the apple sauce, Miss City Slicker," Mrs. Baker said, laughing at her daughter's nonsense.

"When are you going to look for a job, Hill?" Susan asked.

"I thought I might have a look through the paper tomorrow."

"And only answer ads for jobs in the South Seas, I suppose...?"

"Oh, no," Hilary replied, shaking her head vigorously. "I've gotten over that little deviation. As dad said, the air would be far too rich."

FOR TWENTY-FOUR HOURS the rain continued to pour down in slashing, gray sheets. Susan and Hilary sat in the living room the following morning, both intently studying the job opportunities columns in the morning paper.

"Susie," Hilary said suddenly, forcefully circling two compact lines of copy, "have you done any drawing lately?"

"I did a fair bit of painting while I was at Aunt Ruth's, but drawing...?"

"I mean graphic stuff—you know, long, leggy ladies in diaphanous dresses," Hilary said, giggling at her alliteration.

"Not for a while. I've been working mostly in watercolor recently. Why?"

"Because, my dear," Hilary said triumphantly, "here, at the very tip of my pencil, is just the job for you."

"What?" Susan looked incredulously at her sister. "Hilly, you fool, it's you that's supposed to be looking for a job, not me!"

"Listen, Susan," Hilary said, lowering her voice and casting a furtive glance at the living-room door, "this is a brilliant suggestion: stick around here—London, I mean—for a while. Then later, when things you-know-where have cooled down, go back if you want to. This job is free-lance anyway. It's hourly paid according to this ad, and they just want someone initially for three weeks while a staff member is on holiday."

"I...wasn't really planning to stay that long—" Susan began doubtfully.

But Hilary was not to be dissuaded. "It's an ideal solution to your less-than-ideal situation. You need the break, Susan, it will get your mind off—"

"I have my job at the gallery to go back to," Susan protested, but she could feel herself weakening. In fact, she could feel a little bubble of excitement growing in her at the thought. She had never seriously considered being a professional graphic artist. Her primary interest was in oil and watercolors; she had even dreamed of having her own exhibition someday. But graphic art—that was something quite different.

"The gallery need never know," Hilary pointed out reasonably. "For heaven's sake, Susie, it's only for three weeks. You'll have gotten your resilience back by then, and if you then feel like going back to Grasshopper Hill, you'd be free to. Come on," she said, giving her sister a little push. "Phone this number."

A little diffidently, Susan headed toward the phone in the hall, with Hilary, clutching the newspaper, close on her heels.

Yes, the voice on the other end of the line explained, it was the first day the ad had appeared, and yes, they needed someone right away; did she have a portfolio or any experience in the field?

With the receiver cradled in the hollow of her shoulder, Susan held out her hand for Hilary's pencil and began to scribble an address on the corner of the newspaper.

"Tomorrow!" Hilary gasped, the minute Susan hung up the receiver. "Good for you!" Then her eyes grew wide as she said, "What's this portfolio you told them about?"

"I kept all the sketches I did for the exhibits at the gallery, thank goodness, and also one or two of my more inspired pieces from the play we put on during my last year at school."

"Smart lady," Hilary said, nodding her head. "Mind if I tag along tomorrow? Not to the actual interview, of course," she added hastily. "I'll meet you afterward so I can be the first to hear the good news."

"Optimist!" Susan laughed. "I think my 'portfolio' could probably use a few additions; I'll see you later. Right now it's 'artist at work.'"

Susan spent the remainder of the day at the desk in her bedroom sketching furiously. Her interview was with one of the large department stores on Oxford Street. The art department there was looking for a temporary replacement for one of their artists and the job would entail designing and drawing advertisements that would appear in magazines and newspapers. Susan was mindless of the time as she drew sketches of models in the most up-to-date women's and men's clothes, as well as illustrations of crystal and china. She even made a diligent attempt to draw some kitchen appliances, but threw away her tenth piece of sketch paper with what was a mixture of a sigh and a giggle. Her microwave oven persisted in looking like a television, and her Dutch ovens more closely resembled witches' cauldrons. By teatime, however, she had a dozen or so new sketches to add to her portfolio, and with a yawn and a stretch, she finally put down her pencil.

She left her desk and walked over to the window, feeling stiff from the several uninterrupted hours she had spent concentrating on her work. Outside, the rain was still falling, only now it fell in a gloomy, persistent drizzle. A shroudlike fog had descended over the area, and Susan could barely make out the houses on the other side of the square.

Funny, she mused, how things were different in the city.... If she had been at Grasshopper Hill now, she'd have waited until the fog cleared a little bit; then, donning rubber boots and an oilskin, she would have set off for a long walk, accompanied by an exuberant wolfhound. The grass would have seemed especially green after the rain, and all the flowers would be open, drinking in the moisture. The country smells would have become sharper: the hay, the wild flowers, the grass.... In the city, it seemed, rain was just a nuisance, holding up traffic and causing accidents. Idly Susan found herself hoping that the rain would clear before the next day.

Suddenly she realized that she had thought about Grasshopper Hill without thinking about her grisly "mishaps." It was then she knew, beyond the shadow of a doubt, that sooner or later she would have to go back.

THE BAKER FAMILY had just finished dinner that evening when the telephone rang. Susan got up from her chair as she offered to answer it.

"Hi, Aunt Ruth...just fine, thank you...."

"Does my sister miss you already, Susie?" Mr. Baker asked as Susan went into the living room a little later to join the rest of the family for coffee.

"I wouldn't go that far, dad," Susan replied modestly. "She just wondered whether I'd be back for the weekend, as she's having some people over for dinner. I...I told her I didn't know how long I'd be staying in London."

"That wasn't very considerate, dear," her mother reproved gently. "Didn't you give her any idea at all?"

Susan flushed guiltily. "I...told her that there was a small possibility I would be back before the end of the week...."

"But since Susan is obviously going to get the super job she's applied for, that's rather out of the question, isn't it?" Hilary put in breezily.

"Any other news?" Mr. Baker wanted to know.

"Nothing much.... Oh, of course there is! Aunt Ruth's bought a new car!"

"The old Mini finally gave out, eh?"

"Sort of...." Susan mumbled into her coffee. "She bought another Mini; she swears they're the most efficient little cars around."

Mr. Baker leaned over to his wife, who was seated on the sofa beside him and said something to her about trading in their own car. Taking advantage of the diversion created, Susan turned to Hilary and said in a whisper, "Aunt Ruth said she bumped into Lindy Barwick on her way to the car dealership in Farnham. Apparently Lindy said she hadn't seen me around for ages, and she asked what had become of me. You should have heard Aunt Ruth describe the meeting; it was really funny! Lindy seemed to be dying of curiosity to know whether I'd gotten sick or something, and Aunt Ruth wouldn't tell her a thing. All she said was that I'd gone away for a few days—possibly for a lover's tryst—but that she really wasn't sure!"

"Good for Aunt Ruth!" Hilary laughed. "Fancy the old gal spinning a cock-and-bull story like that!" Then her face became serious. "Any, er, developments...?"

Susan shrugged. "She didn't mention anything. Besides, I've only been gone two days."

"Did you tell her about your interview?"

"No. It seemed a bit premature. I'm afraid I don't share your optimism, Hilly. The competition's fierce in that field, you know."

THAT NIGHT the little men with bright-colored pantaloons came back to visit Susan again. The dream was similar to the previous one she'd had, except that there was a macabre twist. The two figures in scarlet trousers were hopping around a shiny new

red Mini, darting under the car from time to time
so that Susan sometimes lost sight of them. Then,
tiptoeing to the back of the car, one of them slid a
bright yellow bomb under the bumper. "That'll
teach you," he screamed in his squeaky, high-
pitched voice. Susan stood mesmerized as she
watched the little figure, then she turned and fled
to her aunt's house. She shouted her aunt's name
as she ran into the kitchen, but Ruth just looked at
her sharply and said, "Don't interrupt, Susan, I'm
telling Lindy why you've gone away."

"But I haven't gone away!" Susan gasped.

"Oh, yes, you have," her aunt replied calmly.
"You just disappeared...."

"No," she shouted. "No, I didn't! No...."

Suddenly another voice broke in....

"Susan, darling, wake up! Susan!" Susan opened
her eyes and saw her mother standing beside her
bed.

For a minute she couldn't speak, the dream was
still so vivid. She struggled to banish the scene
from her mind, but her heart was still pounding
and she still had the feeling of panic that had caused
her to cry out.

Mrs. Baker brushed the damp hair off her daughter's forehead, then sat down at the side of her bed.
The hall light was on and the bedroom door was
open, letting in a shaft of light that outlined her
silhouette from behind. "That must have been a
horrible nightmare you had, darling," Mrs. Baker
said softly. "There's something worrying you, isn't
there? I've been concerned about you ever since
you arrived home so unexpectedly yesterday.
You're pale and exhausted looking—even your tan
can't hide the fact from me." She gave a little smile.
"Do you want to talk about anything?"

Susan and her mother had always been very
close, and the temptation to confide in her was

almost irresistible, but Susan decided resolutely
not to. Her mother would only try to dissuade her
from returning to Grasshopper Hill, and she was
determined to go back—to find out who was trying
to kill her.

"I probably forgot to open the window," Susan
said, trying to keep her voice calm. "I get nightmares sometimes when the room is too hot."

Mrs. Baker looked at her daughter dubiously,
but obviously thought better of contradicting her.
"Well, if you're sure you'll be all right..." she
began doubtfully.

"I'll be fine, mom! Thanks for coming in. Good
night."

Reluctantly Mrs. Baker left the room, casting a
last troubled look toward her daughter before she
disappeared down the hall.

By the time her mother left, Susan was wide
awake. The contents of the dream had receded to
the back of her mind, and she began to reflect on
why, exactly, she was so anxious to return to Grasshopper Hill despite all the fear that waited for her
there. Unless she confined herself exclusively to
the farmhouse, she had no reason to doubt that the
incidents would start occurring again. That meant
that if she went back she wouldn't be able to ride,
couldn't go for walks, couldn't do anything.... And
people were starting to talk about her "accidents."
Susan remembered that just the previous Sunday
her aunt had made mention of the fact. Susan had
taken her paints and sketchbook and had bicycled
over to a neighboring field for a couple of hours
that morning, leaving Hilary gossiping with her
aunt....

When she had returned she found Hilary flat on
her back in the garden basking in the sunshine, and
Aunt Ruth relaxing in a canvas deck chair next to
her, her legs propped up on an egg crate. The

remains of their afternoon tea had been scattered on a tray. The peace and serenity of the scene had stilled Susan's still-sensitive nerves somewhat, and she had smiled brightly as the two sun-worshippers greeted her.

"I think there's one cup of tea left in the pot," Hilary said, leaning negligently on an elbow to peer dubiously into the pot, "Want it, Susie?"

"Hot tea after a bicycle ride in the sun?" Ruth said from the deck chair. "How about some nice, cold lemonade instead?"

"All these tempting offers—it's hard to decide," Susan joked. "But I'll settle for the tea. It sounds good. And besides, that way I won't have to go inside the house and come out again. I'm almost too hot to move."

"In that case, I'll do the honors," Hilary said, raising the old pot majestically and looking around for an empty cup. "Mind using my mug?" she asked, tossing a slice of lemon unceremoniously into the hydrangea at the foot of the garden.

"I hope you realize, young lady," Ruth said lazily, "that some escaped turkey might be getting into that. We'll have lemon-flavored eggs for a week."

"I wonder if we could market them," Hilary mused as she stirred some sugar into her sister's tea. "What do you think, Susie? Would you pay an extra dime a dozen for lemon eggs? They sure would be handy for lemon meringue pie."

"Not to mention egg-flavored lemonade," Ruth said laconically, tilting her face to the sun.

"Enough!" Susan said, laughing. "Thank you," she added, as Hilary passed her the steaming mug of tea. She sipped it gratefully. "Well, what have you two been up to all day? You look like the picture of decadence, lolling around out here in the sun when there's work to be done. What did you accomplish to merit such reward?"

"Listen to that, Aunt Ruth! Thus speaks one who spent an entire morning sitting around doing nothing, just idly holding a brush over a piece of paper.... And she thinks we're indolent!" Hilary looked affectionately at her older sister, then jumped up from her blanket. "I'm going to leave you two right now," she said, excusing herself. "I've got a cake that is probably burning in the oven."

Ruth shifted in her chair. "You know, darling, I'm glad you didn't go to Lindesfarne today. I think it might be a good idea to ease up on your riding for a little while—at least until Rafe can find out if there's anything funny going on at the stables. Whatever the problem is, I'm sure the vet will be able to pin it down fairly soon, and in the meantime—"

"I know, I know— in the meantime, the inside of the turkey coop needs to be painted, the attic could use a good cleaning, and the silver hasn't been polished for at least three hours," Susan interrupted, laughing. She looked at her aunt speculatively. "But what do you mean by 'something funny,' Aunt Ruth?" she asked, nibbling at one of her fingernails.

"Well, things *are* beginning to look a bit odd, aren't they?" Susan shivered suddenly as a cloud blocked the sun for a moment. "And I don't want to worry you, but...well, people are beginning to talk."

Susan stood up suddenly, and pushed her hands deep into her pockets. "People? What people?"

"Calm down, dear, and take it easy. You know I don't set any store by what people say—"

"But it's a small village and news travels fast. Right?"

"Well, it's true. You're not in London now, dear, and people out here have an entirely different idea of reputation than they do in town."

"Reputation?"

"That's right, love. Look at things from their point of view. Within a short time after your arrival, very strange things begin to happen. First Champion is sick, then Tiger. You practically kill yourself at one of Richard's houses, and Richard is famous for being careful on his construction sites. It just looked funny.... What if Richard had gone up those steps first? It would have been logical—he's the host, he would have been leading you around. And then you take me for a drive and, out of all the cars in Farnham—the Mini suddenly is blown up in our faces. Can you understand why some of the villagers are talking?"

The horrible sense of foreboding, which had been haunting Susan over the past few weeks but which she had managed to forget as she visited with her sister, returned in full force with Ruth's words. Susan stared into her aunt's gentle but worried face, trying desperately to calm her pounding heart.

"And you know, dear, it's going to look even funnier if anything else happens. That's why I thought that perhaps you should stick around the house for a little while," Ruth said, trying to gauge Susan's thoughts by watching her face.

But Susan's face was a mask—a mask of fear. She looked around her. Everything was familiar—the cottage with its well-worn brick front; the turkey coops glistening with fresh paint; the kitchen garden drooping a little in the hot afternoon sun. Even Aunt Ruth's benign face.

Suddenly everything had changed. Familiar things could no longer be trusted; familiar faces became the faces of the enemy. It was like a nightmare, where the things most dear were to be feared the most. Susan remembered that, with a strangled cry, she had broken out of her trance and had run into the house, her body trembling.

Chapter 14

Susan shivered and pulled the covers around her more tightly even though the room was warm. She remembered all too clearly the fear that had gripped her that Sunday. And it had been only the next day that she and Hilly had learned from Rafe that Big Tiger had died a slow, painful death....

Why should she ever go back to Hampshire? Perhaps she would get the job she had just applied for, and anyway, there was always the gallery....

Then, unbidden, a small, clear voice spoke from the far regions of her mind: "You're a fool, Susan Baker, if you don't know why you're so anxious to go back. It's not Grasshopper Hill, it's Richard Evans. You're in love with him."

If Susan had held up a mirror at that moment she would have seen reflected an awed but almost curious expression on her face. *Is that it,* she wondered. *Am I in love with Richard?* Her heartbeat was beginning to quicken as she thought back to the times they had spent together and the effect his presence inevitably produced on her. How could she not have realized, she chided herself. Of course! It was so obvious. And cagey Aunt Ruth had known it all along. It had probably been to Richard that she had referred to, talking about her "plan of attack." Aunt Ruth was just like that....

When Susan had sprung up from her chair that evening at dinnertime, and had almost hurled herself at the telephone, had she been hoping that it would be Richard calling? Surely he must know that she'd gone back to London. Was he, in fact, indifferent to her? Gilly had said that he'd been seeing Lindy....

With renewed determination Susan resolved to talk her way into the job in the department store. "That's three whole weeks," she whispered aloud. "I wonder if he'll call me...?"

SUSAN DID get the job, and she was more thrilled about it than she would have thought possible. "They loved my drawings," she told her sister ecstatically, as they lined up at the door of the department store dining room, waiting to be seated. "They hired me right on the spot!"

"When do you start?" Hilary asked eagerly, as pleased as Susan at the success of the interview.

"Monday!"

The mood of the two women was infectious, and that night at dinner all members of the Baker family were particularly jovial.

"Cross your fingers that no one at the art gallery bumps into you, Sue," her mother warned. "They're going to want to know why you're back in town but haven't returned to your old job."

"I can't go back for just three weeks. If I went back there I'd have to stay; my leave of absence would effectively be over. This job is ideal because it's temporary, and I'm free again in three weeks."

"Any plans to see Peter?"

Susan shrugged, at a loss as to how to answer her mother's question. "I'm not sure," she said vaguely. "Our parting wasn't very pleasant."

Mrs. Baker nodded sympathetically. "Well, see how you feel in a few days' time...."

It transpired, in fact, that Susan met Peter that weekend. She and Hilary had gone out to lunch in a Japanese restaurant in Soho. They had passed the morning very pleasantly, window-shopping and looking into a few of Susan's favorite art galleries behind the Burlington Arcade. They had made one or two minor purchases in a few of the stores, and were just piling their various packages on an empty chair when Peter strode into the restaurant, followed by Lindy Barwick's brother, Anthony.

"Susan!" Peter called out delightedly, walking toward the table where she and Hilary were seated. "I'd heard you had come back to town."

"News travels fast," Hilary remarked dryly.

Ignoring Hilary's comment, Peter added, "Anthony, here, told me."

Anthony looked slightly embarrassed, as if he had been caught gossiping. "Lindy called last night, and she mentioned in passing that she thought you were back in London."

"Tired of the quiet life, Sue?"

Susan felt herself stiffen at Peter's question, and she wondered what she could say to satisfy him without explaining to him the real reason for her sudden return to London.

Mercifully, her sister came to her rescue. "I asked her to come back for a few days," she informed Peter nonchalantly. "I missed the competition for the bathroom in the morning."

Peter raised a skeptical eyebrow at Hilary's statement. "Whatever the reason, Susan, I'm glad you're back," he said. "Mind if Tony and I join you?"

"It might be better if you don't," Hilary said quickly, "I've got a filthy cold." She then began to cough furiously, turning her face bright red with the effort. "The English weather, you know," she added, half choking.

"I think, in that case, we'll sit elsewhere," Peter said with a half grin. "See you later."

Susan used every bit of her willpower to stifle the laughter that had been rising in her. "Hilly, that was brilliant," she whispered. "What inspiration!"

"Only a temporary reprieve, I'm afraid. Now that Mr. Wonderful knows you're back, he'll probably call you."

"Mmm," Susan murmured, eyeing the menu. "I'm not much good at thinking on my feet. I'll have to figure out something to tell him before he calls."

"A penny for your thoughts," Hilary said a little while later. "You've worked your way through half a plate of tempura and you haven't said a word. I've asked you three times whether you think I ought to apply for that job in the law firm."

"Hilly, I'm sorry," Susan said contritely, "I was miles away."

"And I can guess in what direction," Hilary commented. "Do you think a bunch of lawyers would drive me crazy?"

"To be quite honest, yes. I think you'd be better off with people as zany as yourself. How about an advertising agency or a theater group?"

"I think you're right," she nodded, sipping her sake. "Now, my offer of a penny for your thoughts still holds good...."

"Since when were Peter and Anthony friends?" Susan asked with a frown. "Anthony's much younger than Peter; I'm sure they weren't friends at school."

Hilary waited as the two men paid their bill, then left the restaurant. "Anthony's only a couple of years younger than Peter. That age spread makes a lot of difference at school, but it doesn't matter after that. Peter mentioned that they both work for accounting firms, and I guess they've had some contact professionally—small world, and all that. Why so curious?"

"Only because I can't imagine Lindy bothering to comment to Anthony on my absence. Why on earth would her brother care about my comings and goings? She must know that Anthony is friends with Peter, and I know I mentioned to her that Peter and I had been seeing each other. I guess she's playing matchmaker."

"I guess she's playing 'Let's get Susan reunited with Peter so I can have Richard to myself,'" Hilary said cynically.

Susan felt her insides lurch and she pushed the remainder of her lunch away distastefully. "So you agree with Gilly? You think Lindy wants the field clear?"

"It seems fairly obvious to me."

"Oh, Hilly," Susan said, her voice low and a little shaky. "Do you know that I've...fallen in love with Richard myself?"

If Susan had been looking to her sister for sympathy, she was disappointed. "High time, Susan," Hilary said briskly. "You'd make a perfect match."

"What good is that?" she wailed. "I'm no competition for Lindy. By Gilly's own admission, Richard's been seeing her! Besides," she added bleakly, "he thinks I killed Rafe's horses."

"How do you know?" Hilary asked with asperity. "Did he say that to you?"

"Well, not exactly," Susan admitted.

"I think you're underestimating him. He's not a fool, you know."

"I know," Susan agreed dully. "Only...that day when we were over there for lunch...and Dr. Fairweather called, he seemed to suddenly grow cold—almost distant."

"If you don't mind my saying so, Susan, I think you were beginning to lose your perspective down there. Those weird occurrences were really getting to you." Hilary reached over and took hold of her sister's hand. "Keep the faith, my dear, I don't think Mr. Evans is lost to you forever."

Susan looked at her sister dubiously. "The eternal optimist," she murmured.

Their lunch over, they both rose and began to collect their purchases. As Susan pulled out her wallet to pay for her half of the bill, Hilary laid a restraining hand on her arm. "Allow me," she said gallantly. "This is my treat, to celebrate the changes in your life."

SUSAN'S FIRST WEEK in the art room of the department store passed very successfully. She learned the ropes quickly, and after a few days began to feel at ease and confident in the environment. She found the work was exhausting, but exhilarating at the same time.

"Why didn't I think of doing this kind of work before?" she commented to her sister the following Friday evening. "I really enjoy it, and working freelance, anyway, the money is really good."

"I think you're something of a purist," Hilary replied absently. "You probably thought graphic art was not 'real art,' or some such nonsense."

"Touché, Hilly; you have a point."

THE FOLLOWING Monday evening, Peter telephoned Susan and invited her out to lunch the next day.

"But I only get forty minutes," she protested, briefly telling him about her new job. "And you work miles away."

Peter informed her that he was meeting a client not too far from where she worked and that they could have a quick meal in the department store cafeteria. Susan agreed hesitantly, still uncertain of what she would say to him regarding her unexpected return to London.

"Relax," Hilary told her casually. "Just tell him what you told mom and dad. You miss the family and you're back for a short visit...."

Peter, however, didn't believe her excuse for a minute. "Oh, come on, Susan," he scoffed. "Since when do you feel all this homesickness? That's not like you; you're an independent spirit. And how well I know it!"

Susan squirmed. "I didn't go on a retreat, you know," she said finally. "I never had any intention of banishing myself. I just had a lovely two months in the country with my aunt, I'm home for a little while now—call it a change of scenery—and I'll go back to the farm in another couple of weeks, probably. My job ends the first week in July."

"Then what?" Peter asked. "How much time has the gallery given you?"

"We didn't really agree on anything definite. It's a fairly relaxed operation in terms of staff relations, and because I've been working there for five years, I guess they sort of trust me not to exploit their goodwill too much. I'll probably be back there by the end of September."

"And what about us, Susan?"

Susan shifted uncomfortably in her seat. She knew that even though Richard would probably never return her love, she could never have a future with Peter—of that she was quite certain. It would be far better to tell him now, she thought, than to put it off indefinitely. She searched carefully for the right words.

"Peter," she began slowly, "I'm not convinced that you and I would make a very good combination. I think we're...looking for different things in life. I'm far more of a country bumpkin than you realize, or are prepared to accept. I'm not at all convinced that I want to spend my life in the city, and it seems to me that if you were really honest about it, you'd agree that you're happiest here in London."

"But, Susan, we can have both. Stop making the situation so black and white."

"It's you and I that are black and white," she said gently. "At least, that's how we seem when we're together. I wouldn't make you a good wife, Peter, and, knowing that, I couldn't enter into a marriage with you."

"I can't understand why you're saying this," Peter said incredulously. "Why, Tony said—"

Susan froze. "What did Tony say?" The words came out in a barely audible whisper.

Peter flushed and self-consciously ran a hand through his hair, feeling the impact of Susan's intense gaze. Averting his eyes from her face, he said quickly, "Lindy told her brother on the phone the other night that the reason you'd returned to London was that you missed me. You'd had a chance to think about our relationship and had had a change of heart. She said that you . . . you wanted to make your peace with me and begin again."

Susan was speechless. So that was the interpretation Lindy had put on Aunt Ruth's nonsensical comment about Susan leaving Hampshire for a lovers' tryst! Lindy had thought she was coming back to Peter! Suddenly Hilary's words echoed in her mind: "Let's get Susan reunited with Peter so I can have Richard to myself. . . ." Well, Susan thought bitterly, how beautifully she'd played into Lindy's hands!

"Peter," Susan said, shaking her head, "I'm afraid that that isn't true. Yes, I did think about our relationship—a great deal, in fact. But the conclusion I reached was just the opposite of what Lindy told her brother. I'm sorry."

"I guess there's no more to be said, then," Peter said, a bleak expression on his face. "I can only hope you know what you're doing."

They were silent as they got up, paid the bill and took the escalator up to the main floor. "Goodbye, Susan. Look after yourself."

Susan's eyes filled with tears as she rode up to the seventh floor of the large store. She felt suddenly very empty, and pleading a headache to her co-workers, she remained silent and wretched for the rest of the afternoon.

That night Susan told her sister about her lunch with Peter and that she'd ended the relationship.

"It's always painful, Sue," her sister said sympathetically, "and what people so often forget is that it's often as painful for the person who's forcing the breakup as it is for the one who's being rejected. You were wise to do it, though; you two weren't right for each other."

"I know," Susan agreed, wiping the tears from her cheeks. "No one likes to hurt anyone else, and I guess I cared more for Peter than I realized."

"Imagine Lindy passing on that barefaced lie to her brother," Hilary repeated incredulously. "The nerve of the woman!"

"A calculated risk, I suppose. If I mention anything to her, she'll probably deny it vehemently and say that her brother misunderstood her."

"She's a devious lady," Hilary said, "and I don't trust her one little bit."

Susan nodded miserably and said that she was inclined to agree.

BY THE MIDDLE of the second week at her job Susan was beginning to think obsessively about Richard. Why hadn't he called? She had telephoned her aunt on the weekend and had asked casually about Richard. Aunt Ruth replied that he hadn't been out to Grasshopper Hill recently, and that she assumed he was very busy with his work. Very kindly she had offered to give Richard a call and ask him over to dinner, but Susan had hastily assured her that that wasn't necessary. Maybe he was away, Susan thought, and she clung to that hope for as long as she could.

But by the end of the following weekend, there had still been no word from him. "He's probably as happy as a lark with Lindy," she told Hilary dismally.

"Then put yourself back on the train to Farnham as soon as you're finished your job." Hilary advised her. "Go and investigate the situation yourself. Do you think you could cope with it—going back there again?"

"In some ways, I'm terrified," Susan confessed. "But I have to see Richard again. I'm miserable here. At least if I went back, I'd know what the situation was between him and Lindy."

Hilary looked at her sister speculatively. "It could be dangerous, Susan. I'm worried about your going back there."

Susan winced at her sister's word. "Don't say that, Hilary. I'm going to assume that I just had three freak accidents—nothing more. I'm sure I was just letting my overactive imagination get the better of me."

THE FOLLOWING FRIDAY, Susan packed her suitcase and took it to work with her so that she could catch the first train to Farnham at the end of the day. She had telephoned her aunt to say she was coming, and she was looking forward to her return to the country with mixed feelings. Part of her was aching to see Richard again; another part was terrified of the possibilities that stretched in front of her. When would the next "freak" accident occur? And under what circumstances?

Susan caught the five-thirty train, and an hour later was being warmly greeted by her aunt. "I've missed you, Sue, and I'm glad you've come back. I'm pleased for my own sake, of course, but I'm pleased particularly that you've found the courage to face the situation back here again. I'm glad you weren't driven away permanently."

They drove back to Grasshopper Hill, catching up on each other's news as they went. As they approached the farm, Susan looked out the window of the shiny new Mini and felt her eyes mist over. *I've come home,* she thought. *With or without Richard Evans, this is where I belong.*

"I nearly didn't get to the station on time," her aunt was saying. "Today seemed to turn out to be chore day, and I've been scooting all over the place, heaven knows where."

"Oh?" Susan said absently. "What have you been up to?"

"Lucy Whilsmith is still laid up, for a start. Her hip hasn't mended properly; the doctor thinks he may have to operate. Anyhow, I took her some library books, then went into Farnham to pick up the butcher's order for turkeys."

"Already? It's only July."

"I know. It seems early, but I have to get an idea of numbers. There's still time for another generation of turkeys to be hatched, if there's the demand. Anyhow, what with that and a few other odds and ends, I only got to the station a minute or two before you arrived."

Soon they were driving down the rutted driveway to Grasshopper Hill. "You know, Aunt Ruth, I'm very pleased to be back." Her aunt gave her a shrewd look that forced hot color into Susan's cheeks. *She knows why I'm back,* she thought. *She knows I'm in love with Richard.* "Where's that crazy wolfhound of yours? Where's my welcome?"

"I expect she's rabbit hunting, or digging in my garden," her aunt said with a shrug. "She'll return in a minute, no doubt, now that she's heard the car."

Ruth pulled the car to a stop and began to extract her parcels and bags from the backseat.

"There's the slothful creature," Susan said, pointing to the suppine form of the dog outside the kitchen door. "Lazy thing, sleeping through my arrival...Willie!" Susan called. "Come and say hello, old girl."

Taking the suitcase her aunt handed her, she began to walk toward the house. "Willie! Where's my greeting?" As Susan drew closer to the dog, she suddenly froze, the suitcase falling from her hand with a thud. The dog's body was absolutely still, its eyes wide open and glazed.

"Oh, my God," Susan whispered in horror. "Oh, no...Aunt Ruth!" her voice rose in a scream.

"What, love? I'm coming." A moment later Susan's aunt was standing beside her, staring at the dog.

"Willie's dead, Aunt Ruth...and I haven't even been back for an hour."

Chapter 15

So it had started already. Besides Aunt Ruth, no one had even known she was coming back. And, yet...someone had to know! Susan felt her flesh crawl with the thought that someone was spying on her, monitoring her every action.

"I'll call the vet," Ruth said hoarsely, after the first stunned shock wore off.

Susan followed her aunt slowly into the house. She felt numb as she mechanically put down her case and walked over to the stove to put on the kettle. Then she slumped into one of the kitchen chairs and let the hot tears stream down her face. Almost against her will, she found her blurred gaze turning back toward the still form of the wolf-hound. *Poor Willie, what did you ever do to hurt anyone?*

"Dr. Fairweather will come over as soon as he can," Ruth said, walking into the kitchen. She, too, had been crying. "I'm going to miss her," she murmured sadly. "Willie and I were friends. We've been together a long time...." She stole a quick look at the prostrate body, then turned away in revulsion.

The vet arrived within the hour, followed by a

white wagon and two young assistants. "Where's the dog?" he asked immediately, and Ruth led him to the back door. He signaled to the two men to go around the back, and then passed onto them Ruth's suggestion that they move the wagon to the end of the drive to get as close to the back door as possible.

A short while later the dead animal had been removed by the two helpers, who had then driven away.

"Come and have a cup of tea, Jake," Ruth said, "or would you prefer a drink?"

The vet decided to have tea, and he sat down with the two women at the kitchen table. The three of them remained silent for several minutes, each lost in sad thoughts.

"Was there any way of telling what happened?" Ruth asked.

"Hard to say at this stage. We'll do an autopsy, of course. I trust you would...?"

Ruth nodded her head. "I think we're all thinking pretty much along the same lines. None of us believes it was an accident."

"I'm sorry about the dog," Dr. Fairweather said quietly. "I was very fond of her, too."

"When will you have a verdict...about the cause of death?"

"Maybe by the end of next week. I'll put a rush on it, but the lab is in London, so there's bound to be a bit of a delay."

When Dr. Fairweather had finished his tea, Ruth walked with him to the front door. "Please let me know what you find out as soon as possible, okay? We're heartbroken about this and anxious to know if there's been any foul play...."

"First the horses, now Willie..." Susan began, as Ruth came back to the kitchen. Then with a sob she covered her face with her hands. "I shouldn't have come back.... I knew all this was going to start again, I just knew it!"

"Maybe," Susan said, turning wet eyes to her aunt, "this maniac is trying to tell me to stay in London."

THE NEXT MORNING both Susan and her aunt came down to breakfast at the same time, Ruth later than usual and Susan earlier. Both were subdued; neither had slept well during the night.

"I didn't sleep until about three this morning," her aunt said wearily. "I kept trying to think who, if anyone, would have known you were coming." She shrugged. "I simply don't know. I think we should try not to drive ourselves crazy thinking about it, however. We'll be hearing from Dr. Fairweather soon enough."

Susan resolved to try to follow her aunt's advice. When breakfast was over and the dishes washed, she took her easel and her paints down to the stream at the end of the property. The July sun was dazzling and Susan found herself squinting as she walked, cursing herself for not wearing a sun hat.

The field adjacent to Grasshopper Hill, owned by the neighboring farmer, was thick with ripe corn, and for a minute Susan stopped to watch it sway in the early morning breeze. It was a lovely sight— rich gold and green. Impulsively she erected her easel right where she was standing, and drew her paints and brushes out of her satchel. At first she couldn't make her fingers move, but just stood there, transfixed at the glorious picture in front of her. Then gradually the shapes began to form on the paper: first the outline of the stalks of corn, the ears, the clumps of earth at their base; then came the detail—wisps of brown fiber, hanging sinu- ously from the opening at the top of each ear.

Susan became totally absorbed in her painting and, as usual, she began to know a certain tran- quility—albeit a fragile one. Her only measure of time was the increasing heat of the sun on the back of her neck. She could feel her long hair begin to stick to her skin, and absently she gathered up the long strands, wound them expertly around her left index finger, and secured the makeshift chignon with the handle of one of her thin paintbrushes. Then, her eyes focused intently on her paper, she began to apply the blue paint for the sky. Susan applied the watercolor with plenty of water, and the sky began to take its space behind the corn field—a beautiful wash of color in several gradations of blue.

More through hypersensitive nerves than from any actual sound, Susan had a feeling she was being watched. She stiffened momentarily, then remembered that her aunt had said she would probably join her midmorning so that the two of them could go for a stroll around the property.

"What do you think of it, Aunt Ruth?" Susan said, surveying her painting with a look of satisfaction.

"It's beautiful, Sue," a deep, masculine voice said quietly.

Susan swung around and found herself looking up at Richard Evans. "Richard...!" she murmured, her blue eyes wide with surprise.

"Why didn't you tell me you were leaving, Susan?" he asked. "Not a word, not a phone call...." Suddenly, without warning, he grabbed her by the shoulders, and his grip was so tight that Susan winced. His voice was no longer gentle as he continued, "And now you're back, without a word...."

"Let me go," Susan said, trying to wriggle out of his hold. Her heart was beating frantically, and she felt, unaccountably, a little afraid of him.

Abruptly Richard released her and let his arms fall to his sides. But he continued to stare at her, his green eyes dark with brooding anger.

"I'm...I'm sorry. Things just became...too much," she said lamely.

"Is that all you can say?"

Susan felt herself growing defensive. What did he care about her departure—or her return? He was probably happy enough with Lindy and, no doubt, relieved that he no longer had to keep on rescuing her. "I wasn't aware you required briefing on my activities, Richard."

"I realize you probably felt a certain embarrassment," he said harshly. "After all, it's not the first time you've done it.... But it didn't work out, did it, and now you're back to mend your heart again."

Susan looked at him quizzically. "What on earth are you talking about?" she demanded.

"Are you denying that you went back to your... your accountant? After all, life in the city must seem infinitely preferable to life out here, what with all the strange occurrences—"

"My accountant? Embarrassed? Richard!" she said sharply, "I don't know what you mean. I don't understand—"

He looked at her impatiently. "For heaven's sake, Susan, don't play the innocent. I know damn well"

"Know what, Richard?" Susan interrupted harshly. "What do you know?"

For an instant he was taken aback by the sharpness of her retort, but Susan could see the anger still smoldering in his eyes, and his expression remained grim.

"I suppose I'm being tactless," he said bitterly. "It's quite clear you have no intention of discussing your fiancé with me."

"My what? What did you say?"

"Your fiancé," he said, almost spitting out the word.

Gradually the light began to dawn on Susan. "Richard," she said, her voice suddenly more gentle, "I don't have a fiancé."

"I guess not, seeing that you're back at Grasshopper Hill."

"That's not why I came back," she protested, averting her eyes. "There was...another reason...."

Richard gripped her arms again, but this time less harshly. Quietly he asked, "Why *did* you come back, Susan?"

More than anything Susan wanted to look into his eyes and say, "Because I love you, Richard Evans, and I've just recently realized it." But Lindy was the woman he wanted, Susan thought bleakly, and not for anything in the world would she subject herself to the humiliation of his pity by confessing her love to him.

"Answer me, Susan."

"I want to know what's happening to me here," she said at last. "I want to know who's trying to drive me away...."

"So do I...."

Susan looked back up into Richard's face, the face she loved so much.

"Did...you hear about Willie?" she asked in a whisper. "It was...so horrible—"

"Yes, that's why I came over. Dr. Fairweather called me last night. I'm sorry I couldn't get over sooner."

"Dr. Fairweather called you?"

"I asked him to keep me informed of any irregular occurrences in the area regarding animals. I wanted to know if what happened to Rafe's horses was just a freak accident, or if, in fact, any kind of pattern was developing. I wanted to know if you were being singled out, or if other people's animals were also being...attacked."

"Has anything else happened?" Susan asked tremulously.

"No."

"I'm not surprised...."

"Sue, I'm desperately sorry about Willie. I'd have

come sooner, but I've been tied up all morning, and
I have to meet someone for lunch in a little while."

Lindy, Susan thought miserably. "Don't let me
keep you then. Thanks for coming over. You'd
better be off now; you mustn't keep her waiting...."

"Her? Keep who waiting?"

Susan bit her lip as she realized the slip she'd
made. She felt herself turning hot with embarrassment and searched desperately for a way to cover
her mistake. "I only mean...." she stammered.

"What *do* you mean?" Richard demanded sharply.

Suddenly reckless, Susan looked up at him and
said, "I presume you're meeting Lindy...."

"Now why would you presume that?" Richard
asked, his eyes narrowing as he looked at her.

"I know you see a lot of her, and it seemed natural that—"

"There are a few things you should know, Susan
Baker," he said seriously. "Things about Lindy and
me. But now is not the time. As I said," he added
coolly, "I'm meeting someone for lunch. Let's go
out tonight for a talk. I'll call for you tonight
around eight, all right? Be ready."

Susan watched Richard stride away from her,
then she began to put away her painting materials.
I'm not sure I'll be able to bear it, she thought. *I don't think
I'll be able to sit there and listen to him talk about Lindy
Barwick.*

AT SEVEN-THIRTY Susan was sitting in the living
room with her aunt, drinking a glass of white wine.

"You're looking super tonight, darling," her aunt
told her affectionately. "I love you in that dress."

"Thank you," Susan said. "I bought it in Greece
last summer." She looked down at her sky-blue and
white cotton dress, so typical of those sold
throughout the Greek islands. The front was bib-
like, and the back consisted of two very long straps

crisscrossed to the waist, then tied around the front. "It's very cool, too. I can't remember wearing anything else for the entire three weeks I was there."

They chatted about Greece for a few minutes, Ruth contributing an amusing anecdote about taking a ride on a recalcitrant donkey in Skiathos. By the time she finished describing how the donkey, once it was finally motivated, had come to a full stop right in the middle of the runway at the island's tiny airport, Susan's eyes were streaming with tears of laughter.

"I'll get it," Ruth said, when the doorbell rang a little later. "You'd better repair your makeup!"

Still laughing, Susan went upstairs to remove the black smudges from beneath her eyes. When she descended again she saw that Richard was laughing, too. Obviously Ruth had filled him in on what they had found so amusing.

"Come on, my lovely," he said, eyeing Susan appreciatively, "I have a table reserved at the hotel."

"We're having dinner?" Susan asked, mildly dismayed. Less than an hour earlier, she and her aunt had made short work of a chicken casserole and a large spinach salad.

"No, not dinner," Richard replied. "Just a drink, I'm afraid, but I particularly wanted a table by the huge picture window that looks out over the pond. It's a lovely night and we'll get a magnificent view of the sunset."

It was only a ten-minute drive to the modest but elegant hotel on the other side of Bordon. The hotel overlooked a rather large body of water that never seemed to be called anything other than "the pond." It was a delightful corner of the area, and Susan had frequently ridden horseback along its banks.

As they sat looking out the large bay window, Richard pointed out two riders who were trotting toward the hotel. "It's a nice ride, that one," he commented casually. Susan murmured her agreement, though her thoughts were far removed from the scene before her.

"Richard," she said hesitantly, "I know you've brought me here for a reason, and I doubt, somehow, that it's simply for the joy of my company."

"Why would you doubt that?" His voice was teasing, but his eyes, Susan noticed, had a guarded expression.

"You said this afternoon that there was something I should know about you and Lindy."

"Ah, yes," Richard said, affecting vagueness, "now that you mention it...."

Even though Susan's nerves were raw with unease and apprehension, she refused to be baited by Richard's teasing. *I know what he's going to say, anyway,* she told herself. *I suppose I'm in no real rush to hear it.*

Susan's tension must have been reflected in her face, because Richard immediately dropped his teasing tone and said to her soberly. "You seem to be under the distinct impression that Lindy and I are, er, having some sort of relationship."

"Yes," Susan muttered, eyes downcast. "I am."

"Just for the record, Susan, Lindy means a lot to me, but not in the way you think. Let's say it has something to do with the past. An old score to settle...."

"You mean—"

"I mean, oh foolish one, that I have only loved one woman in my life, and that's the woman who's now sitting across the table from me!"

"What?" Susan gasped.

"Of course, I don't stand a chance, I suppose, compared to a city sophisticate like Peter Whitelaw," he said, his voice tight.

Susan reached over to grasp one of his hands, nearly knocking over her wine glass. "Oh, Richard, I can't believe you mean that.... The reason I came back to this whole nightmare was to be with you! I love you, Richard. I think I always have. It just took me a little while to discover it, that's all."

"I thought my feelings for you were so obvious, Susan. I felt sure my love for you must have been written all over my face every time I saw you. You can imagine how I felt when I heard you'd gone back to Peter! I had thought you were beginning to feel at home here, and it even seemed possible that you might, in time, come to love a country lad like me."

"I did not go back to Peter!" Susan said vehemently. "What on earth made you think that?"

"Let's just say local gossip."

"Richard, don't lie to me. I know perfectly well you don't take any notice of gossip. Aunt Ruth certainly wouldn't have told you such nonsense."

"Well, she seems to have told Lindy," he remarked dryly.

"Lindy! Oh, Lord, now I remember...." Quickly Susan explained to Richard her aunt's dislike of the other woman and how she'd told her that Susan had gone off to see a "secret love." "So Lindy told you I'd gone back to Peter."

"Yes."

"And that's why you never called me...?"

"Yes...I couldn't bear the thought of you being with him, and there seemed to be nothing I could say that would bring you back."

"And in my fantasies," Susan said softly, "I imagined you phoning me to tell me that you loved me and wanted me to come back."

"God, how many times I wanted to do that...."

"One of the reasons I didn't come back, Richard, was that I thought you were in love with Lindy.

Before I left, Gilly said that Lindy had been by several times to see you and Mrs. Norman—"

"Sarah Norman?" Richard asked quickly. "Lindy came to see her?"

"Yes, Gilly saw her go in through the side entrance of your house, where you have your office. Lindy evidently swore Gilly to silence, but your sister spilled the beans the day that Hilly and I had lunch with you."

"I see," Richard said, frowning. "I'll have a word with Sarah tomorrow."

Susan extricated her hand from Richard's and sat back in her seat, her face flushed with happiness.

"I did see Peter when I was in London, Richard. I told him there was nothing left between him and me. I . . . had discovered that I loved you . . . not him. Once I realized that, I . . . had to come back, if only to find out where things stood between you and Lindy."

"I adore you, Susan, and I want you to marry me. Could you live in the country with a farm lad like me?"

"A farm lad?" Susan giggled. "A Cambridge graduate who's one of the most intelligent, attractive men I know? Could I spend my life with the man I love passionately? Yes, Richard Evans, I think so!"

When Richard escorted Susan to the front door of Grasshopper Hill a little while later, he took her in his arms and kissed her with such intense passion that she felt as if she might faint. "Don't ever leave me again," he whispered. "I don't think I could bear it."

Chapter 16

Susan and her aunt spent the whole of the next morning in the rose garden, picking off the dead buds and pruning the wayward stems. The garden had never looked better. The fruits of Ruth Coleman's labor were a glory to behold. She had roses of every color, from the softest pink to a deep, velvety red. The yellow roses were Susan's favorite, and she paid special attention to those bushes.

"It's a beautiful yellow," she remarked to her aunt as she trained the hose on the base of a bush. "I think I'll have the bridesmaids wear that same yellow, and they can carry bouquets of yellow and white roses—it'll be lovely." Susan sighed blissfully and her aunt turned to smile at her.

"As I said at breakfast, Susie, it was high time you and Richard sorted yourselves out."

With a glint in her eye, Susan turned the hose threateningly toward her aunt.

"Truce!" Ruth said, laughing. "What I really meant was, I couldn't be happier for you, darling. And I'm thrilled you're thinking of having the wedding in the little church in Farnham."

From the house they heard the distant ringing of

the telephone and, handing her pruning shears to Susan, Ruth walked quickly toward the kitchen door. The sound of the phone reminded Susan that she was going to call her parents that evening to tell them her good news. With a wide smile she pictured her sister's reaction. Hilary adored weddings, and she would no doubt invite herself back to Grasshopper Hill to plan the ceremony down to the last detail. Susan's head spun with happy thoughts, and she was absentmindedly spraying more water on her rubber boots than on the rose bushes when her aunt returned.

"That was Stephen," Ruth said a little self-consciously. "He's taking me out for a drive this afternoon."

"Oh? And where is the attractive Dr. Dudding driving you?"

"He wouldn't say; he told me to wait and see."

"The plot thickens...."

"I must say, I'm intrigued," Ruth admitted. "He's coming by at two, so I suppose we might start giving some thought to lunch."

Susan made a salad, which they ate with some leftover quiche, and they were halfway through it when Lindy Barwick appeared at the kitchen door, clad in jodphurs and a short-sleeved T-shirt.

"Hi, Susan, Mrs. Coleman!"

"Why, hello, Lindy," Ruth said coolly. "Come in."

"I heard you were back, Susan, and I thought I'd drop by."

I'll bet you heard, Susan thought, but without rancor. *No doubt on one of your visits to Richard....*

"I thought you might like to go riding this afternoon. I've been out all morning; it's beautiful."

Susan could think of several people whose company she would have preferred, but the temptation to go riding was irresistible. She hadn't been on a horse since....

"I'd love to," she told Lindy. "I'll meet you at Rafe's in an hour."

"My, my, such friendliness," Ruth remarked dryly after Lindy had gone.

"I know you don't like her," Susan said, suddenly being charitable, "and I admit she's not my favorite person, but ever since Richard told me he's not in love with her, I can't help feeling more warmly disposed toward her."

"She's all right, I suppose," Ruth conceded. "I guess I'm a little guilty of judging her by her parents. Her mother is a terrible snob, always putting silly ideas into Lindy's head about making a 'suitable marriage' and having a 'suitable job,' given that circumstances force her to engage in such a crass activity as working for a living. All I can say is, I hope Lindy snatches herself a 'suitable man' before Imogene gets back from Cairo. Damn stupid name, Imogene," she added as an afterthought.

"Imogene or no Imogene," Susan said, smiling at her aunt's last comment, "I think Lindy had set her cap for Richard...."

"She should follow her cousin Jennifer's example and go to Manchester, if you ask me." Then, with a malicious twinkle in her eye, she said, "Better still, introduce her to Peter!"

"Will you be back for dinner?" Ruth asked Susan twenty minutes later, as Susan returned to the kitchen in her jodhpurs and riding boots.

"Of course I will, for heaven's sake. I'm only going riding, not on a cross-country trek!"

Ruth blushed inexplicably. "Sorry. It's just that I thought I'd ask Stephen back for dinner and—"

"And you'd rather I occupied myself elsewhere, right?"

Her aunt looked at her gratefully. "Why not show Richard how emancipated you are by asking *him* out to dinner?"

Susan thought about the idea for a moment. "You know, I think I'll do just that!"

Gilly answered the phone when Susan called the Evans' home. "Susan!" she cried in delight, "Richard told me the good news. I'm *thrilled!*" Susan smiled at Gilly's overemphasis on the last word. "I can't think of anyone I'd rather have for a sister-in-law. Honestly, what a coup! And what a *relief*—" again, the strong emphasis on the last word "—that I'm not going to be related, even by marriage, to you-know-who!"

Susan related her message to Gilly, having first determined that as far as Gilly knew Richard was free that night. "Tell him I'll call for him at eight o'clock," she said, laughing at the role reversal.

When she hung up the phone she said goodbye to Ruth and climbed into the new red Mini. As she drove the short mile to Lindesfarne, she was thinking of her aunt's date with Dr. Dudding that afternoon. Susan hoped that the doctor might be inspired by the news of her own engagement to Richard, and might himself propose to Aunt Ruth. He was quite obviously in love with her, and Susan was certain that if he did ask her to marry him, his proposal would be accepted without hesitation. "Romance, romance," she sang, as she drove up the lane to the stables and got out of the car.

The afternoon was hot and bright, and Susan was glad she had had the good sense to tie back her hair. She had never gone back to retrieve her riding hat after it had flown off during her fateful ride on Big Tiger. Apart from protecting her head in case she ever had a fall, it had also kept her hair out of her eyes. She had meant to go back to collect it, but somehow....

"Come on," Lindy greeted her, "I'm anxious to be off. I've saddled up Pepper Tree for you, to save time."

Susan wondered what the hurry was, but thought better about commenting. *I'm probably a little late,* she thought, *and I'd never call Lindy the most patient person in the world.*

Lindy Barwick, Susan knew, was a very competent rider. She rode with the local hunt club every year, and when she'd been younger she had entered many horse shows and riding competitions in the south of England, usually carrying away with her a good share of winner's ribbons. Though Susan herself was a better than average rider, she knew she never came close to Lindy in skill or competitiveness.

They trotted down the lane leading away from Lindesfarne, and crossed the road heading toward the first of the four adjacent fields on the other side. Lindy nudged her horse into a canter as soon as the ground leveled off, and Susan followed close behind.

"Come on," Lindy shouted over her shoulder. "Let's gallop!"

Susan had often thought with a chuckle that horses, like cars, have four gears, and as she applied pressure to Pepper Tree's side with her knees, she felt as though she were shifting into top gear. The horse's transition into the faster gait was fluid, and a second later Susan was galloping along the open field, feeling the wind rush against her face. It was heaven.

They galloped flat out for about two minutes. Then, at Lindy's cue, Susan slowed the gelding's pace to a canter, to a trot, and finally to a walk. Lindy slowed her own mount to allow Susan to come abreast of her.

"That was fabulous," Susan said, slightly out of breath.

Lindy nodded but said nothing. Susan noticed that she seemed slightly preoccupied.

They were at the far end of the third field, where, off to one side, stood a cluster of small cottages. "Richard is converting one of those houses," Lindy informed Susan. "Why don't we ride over and have a look at it?"

"What about the workmen?" Susan protested. "They may not want us getting in the way."

"It's Sunday," Lindy reminded her. "We won't be disturbing anyone."

Susan agreed that she'd love to have a look around, and together they headed toward the old cottage. Tying their horses to the front fence, the two women walked into the half-gutted house. The windows on the ground floor had been considerably enlarged, and the afternoon sun streamed into what Susan guessed would be the living room. It was largely open plan, and the dining room, facing the back of the house, was separated from the front room by a wall reaching only halfway up to the ceiling.

"It's going to be nice, isn't it?" Lindy commented.

"Richard seems to have done it beautifully," Susan agreed. "Even though the place will be modern, it will still retain much of its original charm."

"I've brought some tea with me," Lindy said after they'd made a tour of the upper floor of the cottage. "It's in the saddle bag; I'll get it."

"That was thoughtful of you," Susan said when Lindy returned. "I'd love a cup of tea right now." She held her hand out gratefully for the top of the Thermos that Lindy had filled. "Aren't you having any?"

"There's only one cup," Lindy replied, pointing to the red plastic container in Susan's hand. "I'll have some when you're finished."

Susan sipped the tea with pleasure. It was sweeter than she liked it, and a little odd tasting—probably from the Thermos, she thought—but it was very welcome, since her throat felt parched from the hot ride. The two women were sitting cross-legged on the living-room floor, contemplating the view of the fields they had just ridden across.

"I envy the owners of this place," Susan commented after a moment. "It has a wonderful view, unimpeded by the other cottages."

"I agree.... Susan, are you all right?"

"Actually, I'm starting to feel a bit nauseous. It's probably indigestion. I must have eaten too quickly at lunch."

Lindy was quiet for a moment, gazing at Susan's flushed face. "Good."

"What?"

"Good. That means the stuff is working."

"Lindy, what *are* you talking about?"

"I'm talking about the chloral hydrate I put in the tea. Knockout drops! Don't worry, Susan," Lindy said coldly, "it won't kill you...I don't think. However, it's supposed to be very, very painful when they pump out your stomach. If they find you, that is."

Susan looked at the other woman in horror, a vague realization coming to her through the waves of dizziness she was starting to feel. "Wh-what are you thinking of, Lindy?" she asked hoarsely.

"To give you a few words of warning and advice, then wait until you pass out either from the pain or the poison."

Speechless, Susan waited for Lindy to continue. Her mind tried frantically to figure out a way to get past the other woman so she could go to the next cottage for help, but her body felt as though it was quickly losing its mobility.

"By the way, Pepper Tree took off," Lindy remarked casually, noticing Susan's anxious look out the window. "I untied him when I went to get the Thermos. I gave him a thump, and that's all the inducement he'll need to head back to the stables. He's hungry, you see. I haven't fed him for a day or two."

"And when you do feed the horses," Susan whispered, the full horror of the situation coming home to her, "you feed them arsenic."

"So you figured that out, did you?" Lindy commented coolly. "Full marks."

"Fowler's solution," Susan said bitterly. "What a sadist you are, Lindy."

"Ouch! Such a harsh word, dear Susan. I would prefer to call it an unfortunate necessity. It did work rather well, though, didn't it?"

"Why, Lindy...?"

"Simple," Lindy replied. "I don't want you around."

"The oasthouse.... It was you who put Andy Norman up to delivering the note...to get rid of the workmen so you could put in the false landing...."

"Right, again. It was messy involving Andy, but it couldn't be helped. But since he owes me a favor, shall we say...."

"It could have been Richard who had fallen," Susan said. By now she was feeling hot and dizzy, and she could feel beads of perspiration on her face. She lifted her arm to brush them away.

"A calculated risk—he's a gentleman, and as they say, 'ladies first.' Fortunately, he was true to form. And it wouldn't have been the end of the world if it had been him instead of you, anyway."

"And the car?" Susan murmured, bending double and dropping her head between her knees.

"Ah, yes, that was my favorite one. I'm sorry I scared your aunt," Lindy went on in a conversational tone, as if she were discussing a horse show or the weather. "The thing is, it was a rather spurof-the-moment idea. I noticed you in the hardware store, of course, and happened to have that little device with me at the time.... The streets were crowded, so no one noticed me slip it under your front fender. But what I didn't realize, you see, was that your aunt was with you. You should have told me," she said, her voice, by its very naturalness, making Susan shiver. "I really quite like your aunt; it's too bad she had to be involved."

"Lindy," Susan said, almost moaning, "if I had thought that you and Richard—"

"That's the trouble, Susan," Lindy interrupted, shaking her head, "you didn't think at all. Why do you imagine I came back to this godforsaken village last Christmas, if not to lay claim to Richard? Really, Susan, you are stupid. Everything was proceeding quite well until you showed up.

"You always did spoil things, didn't you? You couldn't leave Richard alone.... Even when I thought you were all set up with that foolish peacock, Peter Whitelaw, you had to come back to Hampshire."

Lindy's voice had changed to a hard rasp. Through her dizziness Susan numbly recognized the fact that the woman before her had completely changed personality, and that she was revealing a side of herself that Susan had never seen before. "After the car incident I thought I'd finally gotten rid of you, I even tried to work on your sense of guilt by getting Anthony to tell Peter you were coming back to him. I thought that you'd feel badly about having left the stupid man, and that you'd go back to him once and for all."

"Was it you...?" Susan began. Her eyes were closed and her face white. She hugged her arms to her stomach, still bent double. The pain was getting worse....

"The dog, you mean? Poor, slow-witted Susan."

Susan imagined Lindy's smiling at her contempt-
uously. "Of course it was me," she lashed out. "The
arsenic worked like a charm on the horses, and the
warfarin—rat poison—worked like a charm on the
dog. Faster, in fact," she added, and Susan could
hear the satisfaction in her voice.

"Are you getting the message now?" Lindy said
harshly. "Get the hell out of here, Susan Baker; get
the hell out of Hampshire. Richard Evans is mine!"

Susan didn't have the strength or even the
inclination to resist Lindy's strong arms, which,
with the strength of the insane, were dragging her
around the partitioned wall into the kitchen area.
Then she propped a heavy piece of plywood over
the entrance, effectively blocking the exit.

"Just in case you think you might want to move,"
Lindy explained, panting. "I doubt you'll have the
strength, but if you do, you'll never get past this."
With the innocent look of undisguised insanity, she
turned and left the room. The last thing Susan
heard before she passed out was the startled neigh
of Lindy's horse as she whipped her crop across its
flank.

Chapter 17

Susan could feel someone shaking her very gently, and then she heard her name being whispered softly but urgently. Her mind wouldn't concentrate on what was happening, however, and when she opened her eyes, the images before her were blurry.

"You're safe, Susan. We've come to take you home."

Whose voice was that, Susan wondered. Not that it mattered, for she was floating, far away from them. The little men in the bright pantaloons were chattering to her, and she had to concentrate on what they were saying. She wished the other person would stop interrupting her.... Then she was being carried away into the darkness. Idly she wondered where the little people were taking her.

Ten minutes—ten years—later she was being carried into a bright room, where she had to shade her eyes from the glare. The room was familiar....

"Drink this," a firm voice directed her.

"No tea! No—"

"It will make you better, Susan. Drink it!"

Susan drank. She grimaced at the taste of the liquid, but finished the entire mixture.

"Now come into the bathroom," the same voice ordered. "This stuff will make you sick. You're going to stay there until you've emptied your stomach as much as possible. Ruth will be up in a few minutes to put you to bed."

SUNLIGHT BLAZED into the room, and sparrows chirped and twittered at the window. With her eyes still closed, Susan stretched langorously in bed, then kicked off her eiderdown with one foot. Turning over and curling up again, she slept for another few hours. When she woke again, the clock beside her bed said three o'clock.

"Susan, are you awake, darling?" Her aunt's voice came softly across the room.

"Come in, I'm awake."

"I've brought you some tea. How are you, love? We had quite a scare last night, I must say. And how terrifying for you . . . the whole ghastly thing."

"You know, Aunt Ruth, what I really feel is a tremendous sense of relief. I'm not sure why, but I'm convinced it's all over; somehow, the air has been cleared."

"I think you're right," her aunt said quietly. "Richard will be over shortly. He came by earlier today, but I wouldn't let him come up to see you. When he arrives, he'll explain the whole thing to you."

"How he found me . . . ?" Susan murmured.

"Are you hungry? Shall I make you something?"

"I'm starving. I'd adore one of your omelets."

Ruth returned some twenty minutes later with a tray of food, and two steps behind her was Richard. "Susan," he said, striding over to her bed and kissing her. "Darling . . . ."

"I don't know which I want more," she said with a shy smile, "you or the omelet!"

"Food first," he replied quickly, pulling the

dressing-table chair over to the side of her bed.

Susan ate her food ravenously, then settled back onto the pillows. "So you rescued me again," she said softly, turning to look at Richard.

"Thank God I did."

"Tell me every single detail, Richard. How did you find me?"

"Literally, one thing led to another. First, as I told you the other day, I intended to speak to Sarah Norman. You mentioned that Lindy had dropped in to see her. Well, I spoke to her yesterday afternoon. It was Sunday, so I had to call on her at her home. It was quite late, probably around six o'clock, when I got there. I should have gone earlier, but when I phoned in the morning she wasn't there, and then I got into some paperwork. The time just flew by."

He was obviously berating himself and Susan laid a comforting hand on his arm. "Go on."

"It took a while to get Sarah to admit the reasons for Lindy's visits. It seems that she had discovered her son's part in the oasthouse affair and had let fly with Andy. Evidently Mike Wynn has taken her out for a drink the odd time, and she found out from him. Andy, of course, told Lindy that his mother had discovered what he'd done and that he didn't want to have anything more to do with her.

"Lindy then took matters into her own hands and went to see Sarah. She informed her that she had caught Andy stealing on more than one occasion from the hardware store, and in return for her silence, had effectively blackmailed Andy into being a coconspirator.

"Sarah, naturally, was frantic. Though her sense of honesty and decency had tempted her to tell Sheldon about the thefts, she was anxious to maintain the status quo, too. For the first time ever, Andy had a job he was managing to keep, and Sarah, I guess, just didn't want to rock the boat. So Lindy bought her silence, too."

"Was it through Sarah that she found out you and I were going to the oasthouse that day?" Susan interrupted.

"That's right. Well, after I talked to Sarah, I returned home to change for our dinner date." Richard smiled grimly at Susan. "Eight o'clock came and went...then nine o'clock. I called Ruth and she had no idea where you were. In fact, she had called me several times while I was over at Sarah's. My housekeeper knew nothing of my plans except that I wouldn't be in to dinner. Gilly was over at a girl friend's.

"Ruth told me you'd gone riding with Lindy, and I realized right away that meant trouble. After all, since when has Lindy ever asked you to ride with her?" Susan nodded.

"I raced over to Rafe's," Richard went on. "He told me that Lindy had come back several hours earlier but that you hadn't returned with her. Lindy, I gather, had told him that you had decided to walk home or something. He was worried because it wasn't like you to send back your horse by itself, but she told him you'd remembered something that was an emergency. When you didn't come back for the Mini, he really got worried. He was just calling the police when I arrived. I persuaded him to hold off for a little while, saying I thought I knew where you were.

"From Rafe's I went straight over to Lucy Wilsmith's and confronted Lindy, who, cool as you please, was sitting watching television. well, I...I said some pretty unrepeatable things to her, and told her I knew all about Andy Norman. She played dumb for a while and then got really strange, saying she'd done it all for me. She said that you were going to make me unhappy, and that all she'd wanted to do was scare you away. She had never wanted to really hurt you.... It was really ugly. For a while she alternated between waspishness and a sort of frantic pleading." He grimaced in distaste.

"Finally I got her to tell me where you were...and then she really broke down. The woman is absolutely insane, by the way. I wasn't sure for a while if I could even handle her or not. But during the course of our...confrontation, I certainly got out of her a full confession of what she's done. Enough to get her locked up. I took her to the police station on the way to look for you, and two of the sergeants came out with me to help. From there on in it was easy...."

"There's one thing that doesn't fit," Susan said, wrinkling her brow. "How did she know I was coming back?"

Ruth, who had sat quietly throughout Richard's recital, now spoke up. "I'm to blame for that, Susan," she said. "I'm appalled to have to say that it was my doing."

Susan looked at her quizzically. "You?"

"Do you remember my telling you how I barely made it to the station to meet you in time?" Susan nodded. "And do you remember that I said I had dropped some library books off at Lucy Whilsmith's? She asked me to stay for a cup of tea, but I told her I was short of time because I had a number of chores to do before meeting the six o'clock train...."

"That was pretty fast work on Lindy's part," Susan murmured. "She couldn't have had much more than a couple of hours. And such immediate inspiration, too," she added bitterly. "How did she think she would get away with it?"

"I don't think that worrying about being caught was part of her pattern. Psychotic people sometimes do incredibly blatant things. With that icy but innocent look in her eyes...." Richard paused a moment and shook his head.

"You'll have to make a statement to the police, of course," he went on. "And if the case ever comes to court, you may have to be a witness. But I don't think it will. I think she'll be sent to a psychiatric prison without much of a delay. There's enough evidence in my report alone to have her held indefinitely, even if she pleads not guilty."

"I hope so," Susan said with a little shiver. "So my statement to the police, and any charges I might want to lay, would be for the record, so to speak."

"That's right," Richard nodded.

"I'm sorry about Lindy, but glad for the rest of us. I think this calls for a celebration," Ruth said, rising from her seat at the end of Susan's bed. "Don't move, either of you; I'll be back in two minutes."

"It's such a relief to have it all over, Richard," Susan said with a sigh. "I think we've all had just about as much as we can stand."

"Especially you, my darling," Richard murmured, and leaned over to kiss her. When Ruth returned bearing a bottle of champagne and a tray with three glasses on it, Richard's arms were still around Susan.

"Let me do the honors," he said, taking the champagne bottle from Ruth's outstretched hand. He unwound the twisted metal from three sides of the plastic cork, then, with his thumbs, applied pressure under its base. "Look out," he called, pointing the neck of the bottle toward the open window. With a loud pop the cork flew out, and Richard quickly wound his handkerchief around the bottle top.

"Don't mop it up!" Ruth laughed, putting a glass under the foaming liquid.

They drank to one another's good health, safety and happiness, each of them offering a different toast.

"There's one more thing," Ruth said, a twinkle in her eye. "Hold on." She disappeared from the room, returning a minute or two later with a large, floppy wolfhound puppy in her arms.

That was the last straw for Susan's precarious emotions. She began to cry as she looked adoringly at the puppy, which her aunt had deposited on her bed. "You gorgeous thing," she said, stroking its silky back. Half laughing, half crying she turned to her aunt. "He's the most adorable dog I've ever seen! When on earth did he arrive?"

"It's a she. Stephen drove me to the kennels yesterday," Ruth replied, "and when I saw her, it was love at first sight."

"What will you name her?" Susan asked softly, watching the puppy tenderly as the little thing began to nibble the edge of the blanket.

"Willie, too, I think."

"Willie Two?" Susan quipped, and laughed with the others at her own joke.

"And, because all good things are supposed to come in threes, there's one more thing I should tell you." From the pocket of her cotton skirt, Ruth extracted an exquisite sapphire and diamond ring, which she slipped onto the third finger of her left hand.

"I knew it!" Susan cried. "Oh, Aunt Ruth, congratulations! Good for Dr. Dudding!"

"I guess you could say, love, that it's high time I got *myself* sorted out!"

Susan held out her arms to her aunt and gave her a hug. "Two weddings," she murmured blissfully. "What heaven!"

"Aunt Ruth!" she called out a moment later, a warning note in her voice. "I recognize the signs. I think you'd better take our new friend outside... quickly. With her eyes wide, Susan was watching in consternation as the puppy began to circle around one small area of the bed.

"Come on, you," Ruth said to the puppy, gathering it up in her arms. "Off we go outside." Her aunt was, Susan decided, in her element. She was at her best when she had someone or something to look after: Susan, the turkeys, the garden...and now a little dog that needed housebreaking.

Richard took one of Susan's hands in his own. "Now that the mysteries are solved—" he began, but Susan interrupted.

"All but one mystery. You told me the other day out in the field that you and Lindy had an old score to settle. What was that all about?"

"When you first came back, we met in Farnham, remember? I bought you tea and fell in love with you again."

Susan nodded. "As if I could ever forget!"

"You asked me how I hurt my leg...why I limped...."

"You told me about your riding accident," Susan said softly, wondering where Richard was heading.

"I did...of sorts. I told you that someone had taken a crop to the back of my horse...and that's why my horse stumbled...."

"Lindy!" she whispered, appalled.

"I had always suspected as much."

"Richard," Susan breathed, "how horrible...! You could have broken your neck. You could have been killed...."

"When I was talking to her, it all came out. She said she had just wanted to cause a mild fall," he continued. "Then she could come over and nurse me. I couldn't believe it, looking into her eyes, Susan! Why, we practically grew up together, and I never knew she had this whole other side to her. Something in her must have snapped while she was away all those years. By the way, the police got hold of her parents' address, and Colonel Barwick is flying back as soon as he can."

"I'm so glad this whole horrible mystery is solved, Richard," Susan murmured. "But I have a feeling that everything's going to be all right now. If Lindy gets into a place where she can get professional help.... And who knows, you might even get all the strength back in your leg, if you ride more often. But even if you don't," she whispered, winding her arms around Richard's neck and drawing his face toward her own, "it's not really important. What is important is that we have finally stopped working at cross-purposes, and have discovered our love for each other. And—"

"And you're talking too much," Richard muttered, and covered her mouth with his own.

MYSTIQUE BOOKS

Experience the warmth of love...
and the threat of danger!

MYSTIQUE BOOKS are a breathless blend of
romance and suspense, passion and mystery. Let
them take you on journeys to exotic lands—the
sunny Caribbean, the enchantment of Paris, the
sinister streets of Istanbul.

MYSTIQUE BOOKS

An unforgettable reading experience.
Now...many previously published titles are once
again available.
Choose from this great selection!

Don't miss any of these thrilling novels of love and adventure!